Death
&TAXES

Death & TAXES

Beating One of the Two Certainties in Life

Revised and Updated Edition

Edited by

Jerry White

Warwick Publishing
Toronto Chicago

Death and Taxes: Beating One of the Two Certainties in Life
Revised and Updated Edition

© 1998, 2000 Jerry White

Revised and updated edition, March 2000

We acknowledge the financial support of the Government of Canada through the Book Publishing Industry Development Program for our publishing activities.

ISBN 1-894020-79-0

Published by Warwick Publishing Inc.
162 John Street
Toronto, Ontario M5V 2E5 Canada
www.warwickgp.com

Distributed in Canada by
General Distribution Services Limited
325 Humber College Blvd.
Etobicoke ON M9W 7C3 Canada

Design: mercer digital

Printed and bound in Canada

Contents

Preface

With a progressively aging population and 5.7 million people in Canada over 55, there is a clear need for information and education on what to do in the post-retirement period of one's life to maximize wealth, as well as how to preserve the capital of the estate.

Our research, conducted in January and February of 1997 of Canadians over 50 as a first project for the non-profit research foundation The Canadian Institute for Personal Finance, shows that only 40% of Canadians over 50 still work; that the average national retirement age is 61 and declining; that only 1% of those over 50 are rich, 8% are well off, 15% are financially secure, 33% have assets in excess of $150,000, 15% must work after age 65 because they need the money to survive; and 82% of women over 65 and 54% of men rely totally on government sources for their income.

It is our belief that knowledge and understanding are critical to empower mature Canadians to take back their financial future. It is our view that we have never lived so long as a people and planned so poorly for it. We must address the pre-estate/post-retirement period as well as estate planning. This is a concurrent exercise that must be addressed by all Canadians 50+, and the failure to alter our behaviour after age 50 as investors, savers and financial custodians of our family's wealth can result in the impoverishment of most and the destruction of assets we have worked our lives to create. It is about taking charge and control — planning, strategizing and succeeding in a dynamically changing financial world and tax environment. It is about personal responsibility, a long-abdicated national issue.

Our goal in the chapters ahead was to assemble a top-level, national team of qualified experts and knowledge providers capable of creating a concise but effective package of ideas and concepts that will be relevant to most Canadians.

The theme of this book is simple: wealth maximize throughout your retirement and simultaneously plan to preserve the wealth you create through planning, expert advice and proper investing. Be flexible and consider all the options. Involve the entire family, and remember: we are only the custodians of these assets for the generations of our family yet to come. We can contribute to our children's, grandchildren's and great-grandchildren's future by what we do today to ensure a secure tomorrow.

In developing this work we had the support of all our qualified contributors, as well as the Canadian Snowbird Association, Mark Simone and Ross Quigley of Medipac International.

The ideas and concepts were tried and tested by us in over 400 public seminars in various forms, such as "Is there Life After RRSPs?" and "Ultimate Wealth, Ultimate Security." This testing was done in all ten provinces over the past five years.

This book is meant to be a body of knowledge to be used by the public in conjunction with expert professional advice and not in isolation. Seek out the services of a qualified estate planning lawyer, tax accountant, estate planning insurance professional and qualified financial planner or broker. They are an invaluable and necessary aid to ensure the successful implementation and execution of the process.

However, this is but a body of knowledge, and knowledge without action is nothing. Take back your financial future now!

Jerry White
April 2000

Chapter 1
Pre-Estate Wealth Maximization
— Jerry White —

We Are Living Healthier and Longer

When we consider the study "Report on Health of Canadians" of 1996, and the U.S. proceedings of the National Academy of Sciences conducted by Duke University, we find we are living longer without disability and we are living healthier as well. In 1970, 40% of seniors over 65 said they limited their daily activities because of health problems, and today it is down to less than 20%. We are spending 90% of our total lifespan free from disabling health problems — the reversal of the "rocking chair" syndrome.

In addition, we are living longer than we planned. Researchers in the Health Canada study found that those who were more financially secure and who had better control over their retirement income were more likely to have less financial stress, conduct pro-active healthcare activities, have better nutrition, and therefore live longer and healthier.

Apparently the belief that money can't buy you health and longevity is simply unfounded. In fact, there is a direct correlation between physical health and financial health — essential fiscal responsibility produces physical longevity.

Those who are less well housed and less well fed are less healthy. Good retirement incomes give us more choice, more freedom and more healthcare options. "Health increases at each step up the hierarchy in income, education and social status," the report says.

With 5.7 million Canadians over the age of 55 and 1.2 million households headed by people over 65, we are at a unique point in Canadian demographic history. By the year 2003 it is estimated that the number of Canadians over 65 will have reached over 7 million, nearly double the number of Canadians under 18. This major demographic bubble has enormous implications for us economically, socially and culturally.

While the average retirement age in Canada this year is just 61, it is expected to decline to 58 in five years. We seem to be living longer and working less. Retirement is just about equal in duration to our working lives. It is projected that by 2120, on average Canadians will spend one-third of their lives in school, one-third working and one-third in retirement.

Unfortunately, never expecting this longevity, most Canadians start saving too little, too late, and end up running out of money before they run out of retirement.

We must combine this "threat" of longevity with the introduction of government clawbacks on Old Age Security, reduced RRSP contribution levels and room and cutbacks on domestic and out-of-country healthcare coverage.

According to the Fraser Institute, taxes at all levels have had a combined increase of 1167% since 1961. While many provinces are continuing to cut personal tax rates, CPP premium increases, the loss of the indexation of tax credits, exemptions and deductions (only restored in 2000) for the past seven years while inflation is under 3% and the inception of the GST (or Harmonized Sales Tax in some provinces) have more than offset provincial reductions. When we look at net after-tax disposable income, the average income of those over 65 has declined by $3,000 in the past four years. Mind you, this was also partly due to the investments held by retirees in such vehicles such as GICs and savings bonds and 40-year-low interest rates.

The Objective
The objective of this book is to look at the retirement process/estate planning as a combined activity, because the interrelationship is critical. Retirement income planning and estate planning are concurrent exercises and inseparable. For an adult male aged 65 we plan until age 90 and for a female to age 96.

If you are over 45 and have not begun your retirement income planning you have a problem. If you are over 45 and have substantial assets, your requirements for estate planning make your situation even more difficult. If you are retiring and accepting a lump-sum payment or retirement allowance, consider immediately planning your estate to protect your family and spouse.

Our research shows that less than 41% of Canadians nationally over 40 have done any estate planning, and for those who have, it usually consists of little more than a will or spousal beneficiary in an RRSP. This will prove to be grossly inadequate. To be successful in your mature years you must address many issues in the planning process (and it is just that — a dynamic process that evolves according to your changing needs and life stages):

- When will I retire?
- How much money will I need to maintain the lifestyle that I want?
- Where will I live — in Canada or elsewhere?
- Will I need supplementary health care?
- Will I ever have to consider part-time work?
- Will my pension sources be adequate for my needs?
- What should be in my portfolio in my pre-estate period and what should my investment goals be at this stage?
- How can my assets be protected?
- How can I continue to grow my capital?
- How can I include my spouse/family in this process for income splitting, taxation and estate planning?

What the Rich Do — Lessons We Can Learn from Our Previous Study
- Invest 20% of your income annually. It is easier to earn income than to accumulate wealth. Investment income should equal 20% of your total income by age 55.

- No home with a mortgage two times greater than annual income.
- Spend 7% of your net worth on lifestyle, e.g., (Net Worth of $500,000) x 0.07 = $35,000 a year
- Net worth should be your age times your pre-tax income divided by ten, e.g., 40 (Age) x $150,000 (Income) = $6 million/10 = $600,000 (Net worth)

Your Assets

- Hold 60% in transactions securities — equities and mutual funds.
- Hold 20% in your home and hard assets.
- Hold 20% in your private pension savings.
- Save at least 15% of earned income annually.
- Spend 2–4 hours a week on planning, managing assets and investments.

Cornerstones

- Thrift, or frugality, wins.
- Discipline is essential in lifestyle, saving and investing.
- Invest, do not lend. Spend the time, and plan.
- Buy and hold. Focus on non-taxed capital appreciation.
- Education and entrepreneurship — the two best investments. Educate your family and be entrepreneurial.
- Financial independence is more important than displaying social status.

Result

Financially independent people are happier, live longer and are healthier than those who are not financially secure.

Pre-Estate Wealth Maximization

One conclusion we have come to is that we must not only do estate planning, but also post-retirement, pre-estate wealth maximization. This is to ensure we do not consume our capital before we die. There is no point to estate planning ("Intergenerational Asset Transfer") if there is no estate left to transfer.

This is a new phenomenon brought on by the fact that if you are 60 today you will probably live to age 90 and have a reasonable chance at 100. This has never happened before in our history and the situation will only get better in terms of aging and worse in terms of seniors in poverty.

At the same time, we must all recognize that we are merely custodians of our family's wealth, just as we are perhaps custodians of the environment while we are here on earth. This means it is our responsibility to preserve the capital we have worked our entire lives to create to enrich the next generations of our family to come. We must be diligent and responsible custodians to ensure that we transfer the maximum amount intergenerationally, but at the same time secure for ourselves a happy, enjoyable, worry-free retirement.

This means that we must practice a constant vigilance over threatening changes, taxes and regulations, while looking to new strategies to grow wealth. The accumulation of wealth must not end at retirement or you will become a capital destroyer. It must grow at a rate faster than its consumption.

If you consume your capital at 8% per year you must have a net after-tax growth of at least 8% or more. Putting a 5% GIC in a RRIF then drawing money at 7.36% means the RRIF will start to decapitalize by age 71.

The Stages of Retirement

Age	Asset Structure	Insurance	Business	Legals	Investing	Real Estate
60-65	10% cash, 50% + equities, real estate, hard assets, bonds.	If not insured, get it right now. Determine size of estate and liability.	Succession plan. Estate freeze. Sell.	Revise will, powers of attorney, trusts.	Buy and hold wealth building.	Downsize. Invest the difference.
65-75	Still a growth period. Consider systematic withdrawal for income, RRSPs for grandchildren, in-trust accounts.	76% of those 60-80 qualify and get approval.	Final decision and planning time. Release the equity to the next generation.	Reviews every 3 years. Healthcare and financed power of attorney critical.	Cash flow not income Annuities systematic withdrawal 100% insured mutual funds	Retirement property in kid's name Use trusts.
75-84	You can still grow capital until age 79. Small reductions in equity holdings, downsize real estate.	Last chance and it won't be inexpensive.	Nothing wrong in working, just let the family be in charge.	Time to have a living will as well.	No speculation. It's cash flow.	Be a snowbird; rent.
85+	The income period. Now's the time to gift assets, reduce the estate.	It's too expensive unless you are very rich.	It's up to you; it keeps the brain dynamic.	Last revisions	Most conservative period. No risk.	30% will consider retirement home, then nursing home.

None of the traditional financial planning processes can alter this. They must be changed to reflect the next stage of your life cycle. This next stage begins at retirement and is finalized at the point of RRSP rollover to the RRIF or annuity. Every stage of the post–55 to 60 era represents a transitional period. The process is one of evolution over time, not a collection of sudden stages.

Throughout this book we will try to address each of these transitional periods strategically to maximize your knowledge and success potential. We have assembled some of the best minds in the business — lawyers, accountants, investment strategists and estate planners. We will also include Canada/U.S. and international issues to ensure most case scenarios are covered.

In the next section we will look at wealth- and income-generation in the pre-estate process and the key decisions we need to make. Remember too that only knowledge combined with action can make a difference. Only *you* can change your financial future, cut your taxes, enhance your returns and preserve your capital; we cannot.

Pre-Estate: Cash Flow Is King, Growth Is Essential
The government provides an indigent couple with income equivalent to having a $250,000 RRSP on a tax-free basis. Yet it still guarantees a lifestyle and income below the poverty line.

The government has recommended that to avoid clawbacks on your OAS you should start to withdraw capital from your RRSPs after age 55 and stop contributing. The government now requires you to report world assets held outside of Canada in excess of $100,000 on a special reporting form.

The government has introduced a Migration Tax Law on your capital if you wish to leave Canada, a capital gains tax on stocks, bonds and business assets that must be paid prior to leaving.

Will any of these things contribute to your financial security? The answer, of course, is no. The government wishes, it seems, to encourage people to withdraw money from tax-deferred plans to tax it now or prevent its growth, or to encourage people not to put away money for retirement. The 1996 RRSP rate changes made it clear they wished to discourage RRSP use and personal responsibility by the middle and entrepreneurial classes. The government has decided to seize 9.9% of the income of younger Canadians so they can "invest" it as they see fit through CPP premiums.

They deem you to be unfit to make such decisions, despite their abysmal track record. The government also says you can't take your money and leave until you pay your taxes.

Universality of benefits is dead forever. The CPP is not a tax, it's a premium, and the provinces' probate-fee increases are not taxes but fees. Yet the Supreme Court ruled Ontario's probate fees as unconstitutional.

Taking money offshore and investing it is being limited to the very well-off with capital in excess of $500,000 and $250,000 in investment dollars, as well as those who can afford the professional fees.

If you wish to be a "snowbird" you must have the money to cover the healthcare costs, which dramatically reduces the number of people who can afford to go south for part of the year.

Low growth, low inflation and low interest rates mean that low returns on fixed income products will be a pragmatic reality of life, long term.

Therefore, in this new era the pre-estate period is now the most financially challenging and dangerous period you may ever face. Tax shelters have been eliminated or substantially limited. Real estate is not the store of value it once was. Choosing to do nothing about this can only be disastrous and a guaranteed path to poverty. What can we do and what must we do?

Income and Anti-Clawback Investment Options

The unique challenges facing us over the next 20 to 30 years are the longevity factor, our lack of preparedness for this longevity, and the changing market/investment and benefit framework.

Today we are confronted with clawbacks on Old Age Security. How do we avoid these clawbacks? Now we have user fees for some healthcare services and progressively higher tax rates. We have lost RRSP contribution room and we see low inflation and low interest rates as long-term phenomena. Inflation will not be there to bail us out of our debts. Real estate, as we said earlier, is not the store of value it once was.

Pre-estate wealth maximization to maximize intergenerational asset transfer is our primary goal. Before we do estate planning we must learn how to grow the capital of our estate at least until age 79.

Longevity

Canadians will live longer than anyone in the Americas and are in the top five in the world in life expectancy. For the sixth year in a row Canada was rated by the United Nations Human Resources index as the best place on earth to live. Yet in 1999 there were more Canadians living below the poverty line than at any other time in the post-war era.

After a 30-year growth of the social welfare state Canadians gave up trying to fend for themselves and chose a life of government cheques over control and freedom based on their own financial resources. We developed a massive sense of entitlement instead of taking on personal responsibilities and maximizing RRSP and retirement savings and investment. We have $240 billion in unused RRSP contribution room. Canadians fear clawbacks in pensions and loss of government cheques more than any other financial threat.

We're Conservative

No, we are not. A conservative investor knows what risk is: it is the loss of capital. A conservative investor knows that a negative cash flow from investments consumes capital. Ever-increasing taxation combined with inflation has produced a massive consumption of capital in the past 10 years. There has been no indexation of credits or exemptions for seven years, causing taxes to rise by $1,350 per household federally. The capital gains tax on estates is their greatest new source of income.

Ten years ago Canadians stood to transfer $1 trillion intergenerationally to children and grandchildren. Today it is closer to $670 billion. The rest has been consumed, put into bad real estate or taxed away.

"We are conservative," Canadians say, yet they have money in daily interest savings accounts at 0.1% while paying 18% on their credit cards. They have the following:

- $34 billion in savings bonds
- $65 billion in savings accounts
- $80 billion in chequing accounts
- $20 billion in money market funds
- $444 billion in GICs

Why are none of these truly conservative investments as we were once misled to believe? Simply, most deliver a negative cash flow after tax and inflation. None are tax advantaged and most do not work in today's low-inflation, low-interest-rate longevity environment.

A savings bond is not a bond, it is cash — a savings certificate. It cannot rise in value if interest rates fall like a corporate bond or Government of Canada 10- or 20-year bond, providing a capital gain to offset the interest loss.

For example, the 10-year variable rate 4.4%, 10-year compound interest bond of 1999 pays nothing for 10 years, yet you are required to report the accrued interest each year for 10 years and pay tax annually — an interest-free loan, or the money you don't get for 10 years guaranteeing a negative cash flow for 10 years. Hence the risk — the loss of capital at -2.2% a year.

GICs are also a negative cash-flow vehicle. Why? Because if held outside of a registered investment such as an RRSP or an RRIF, they have historically generated a negative return. If the average five-year GIC paid 9.4% in the 1970s, after tax and inflation the cash was -3.1% per annum. In the 1980s the average GIC paid 11.2%, but after tax and inflation -0.8%. The return in 1998 was 0.78% cash flow. Indexed GICs are not indices. If they were, the income would be treated as a capital gain and be tax reduced. When you buy an indexed GIC you are not paid anything for up to five years, but you must report the return annually and pay a tax for up to five years on money you have not yet received — a five-year negative cash flow.

Mutual funds are Unit Income Trusts. All mutual funds must distribute all of these earnings at the end of each year. This is a tax distribution producing T3 and T5 reporting slips for tax purposes. If you are on a pension this would produce an OAS clawback. Therefore, the tax efficiency of your investment is very critical to your success in retirement.

Anyone over 60 should seriously consider whether they can afford to be in mutual funds that trade and transfer their tax liability to you. You should ask your advisor about the tax efficiency of your investments first and foremost.

For example, if you are in a fund that trades year round, the tax efficiency of the fund could be as low as 50–60%. This means that whatever the reported returns of the fund, you must multiply it by its tax efficiency to see what you actually received. If the fund reported a 9% return and is 66% tax efficient, you actually got 6% on your money, because of the tax liability transferred to you.

A number of funds are quite tax efficient and rarely trade their portfolio. So they try to hold a limited number of investments that they are extremely confident in. Fidelity True North in 1999 was 100% tax efficient, AGF Canada 100% in 1999, AIC Advantage I & II 100% tax efficient, and the Infinity Mutual Funds have been designed to be buy-and-hold permanent ownership funds that have minimal trades or distributions. Many others trade aggressively. Market timers, stock pickers, sector rotators and momentum players do this regularly. Some have hundreds of transactions.

"But I need income — sorry, I mean cash flow; I can't afford to buy and hold." In some ways you're right and wrong at the same time. You do need cash flow, but we have strategies to achieve it at low capital risk.

Risk

First, let's expand a bit on the nature of risk.

Volatility is not a measure of risk and I have no idea why newspaper writers (they're certainly not financial experts, just people hired to write; if they were experts they would have money, which few or any ever will) talk about the volatility of a mutual fund as an important risk issue. Back in 1992 a number of financial journals carried research clearly showing the degree by which a stock or mutual fund goes up and down in comparison to the market — its volatility was not a measure of risk. Mutual funds that move up or down more than the market are no more or less risky than ones that rarely move at all.

"Risk is in equities. No risk in fixed income!" We have tried to show you that capital risk rests in the non-performance of fixed income which results in a negative cash flow. But what about equities and equity mutuals versus GICs? For example, a 20-year study of mutual funds versus GICs shows that Canadian equity funds from 1971 to 1996 gave us a 12.9% return versus 9.6% in GICs. When we factor in U.S. equity and Western European funds the return was three times greater than that of GICs. This is based on holding the investments and not trading.

What about asset allocation and bonds? Asset allocation has little validity: about 10% of your return or assets should be in cash, treasury bills and savings and savings bonds — all cash instruments for emergency cash needs as we grow older. But what about the remaining 90%?

Conventional wisdom in asset allocation in the 1970s, '80s and early '90s said that for those over 60 the best structure (most capital conservative) was 10% in cash and a ratio of 3:1 of bonds and GICs over equity. In other words, 75% of the remaining portfolio in bonds and GICs and 25% in equity mutual funds. In the March 1997 issue of the *American Economic Review* and in the June 1997 *Economist,* three researchers from McKinsey

Consulting, Brown and Harvard Universities concluded that the exact opposite was true. The ratio should be 3:1 equities over bonds.

The most conservative portfolio therefore is 10% in cash, 67.5% in equities and 22.5% in bonds. Bonds move in conjunction with cash and interest rates. Blue chip equities, especially those with dividends, are also tax-preferred investments. Therefore, while we already knew we needed equities for RRSP and especially RRIF growth, we now see we need even more than we expected.

Professor Roger Ibbitson of Yale in 1997 published a paper on hard-asset investing using oil and gas investments, commodities, gold, REIFs and real estate (as distinct from financial assets), equities, bonds and cash.

When asked to look at the Canadian scene, Ibbitson suggested that having about 10% of the portfolio in oil and gas development partnerships, flow-through shares and royalty income trusts could reduce total portfolio risk by as much as 20% because hard assets tend to perform contra-cyclically to financial assets and act to buttress the portfolio against market risk and inflation/interest rate trends. Therefore, our recast portfolio starts to look more like this:

Cash:	T-bills, deposits, savings bonds	10%
Hard Assets:	REITS, royal trusts, flow-throughs	5–10%
Bonds:	corporate, bond funds, utilities, Gov. of Canada 10–20 year, provincial bonds	20%
Equities:	blue chip major Canadian, U.S., Western European, and equity and mutual funds in these categories	60%
		= 100%

Equity allocation is therefore most critical.

Everyone's Situation Is Different

Everyone should have a custom equity allocation plan prepared to reflect their situation. Everyone has different needs, levels of knowledge, experience, education, expectations and risk preferences. Therefore, custom allocation is critical, but remember the model. Move as a general rule of thumb. In our study of "What the Rich Do" we found that 45% of those over 65 who were rich had 60% or more of their portfolios in equities and equity mutual funds. We saw similar numbers in the U.S. best seller, *The Millionaire Next Door.* Clearly there is substantiation for this proposition of risk mitigation as we now know it.

But What About My Cash Flow?

The following describes what we call the hierarchy of cash flow. We have a number of cash-flow options that are more tax efficient, tax reduced or tax deferred, as you can now see. There are also a number of strategies that help reduce clawback potential. These include

ઢ Royalty Income Trusts

- 28 listed on TSE since 1999
- cash flow payable monthly; taxable only when sold, then treated as a capital gain
- average cash flow 12%

ઢ In-Trust Accounts

- for minor children, grandchildren for capital gains
- avoids attribution from interest and dividends
- establish a Bare-Trust — invest for gains; child needs S.I.N.
- shelters up to $11,000 in capital gains a year per child to age 18

ઢ Self-Directed RESPs

- up to $4,000 a year per child or grandchild + 20% CESG federal grant.

ઢ Buy and Hold Mutual Funds with no distributions

- over 200 now available

ઢ Systematic Withdrawal Plans

- from buy and hold funds

ઢ Universal Life Insurance

- borrow from the policy and the cash flow is not taxable income

ઢ Segregated Mutual Funds

- use to guarantee the capital as you age

All of these investment tools are available from independent brokers or financial planners who can custom design a cash plan for you based on your needs.

Avoid using your home for leveraging or cash. Some intellectually challenged writers have said it is a good idea to borrow against your home as it is a poorly performing asset, but these are the same twits who promoted real estate to begin with. Then, once you've spent 25 years paying it off at a horrific cost, leveraging against it is the epitome of risk for retirees or pensioners. If you borrow for income, the interest expense will not be tax deductible.

You can see I wouldn't be a fan of reverse mortgages either. If you ever borrow against your house, borrow no more than 20% for blue-chip investment only. But then, if they are blue chip, the lender will want *them* as collateral, not your house. If you are in such need of cash why not sell the house? Downsize your housing requirements and costs, buy a small condo or retirement residence, and invest the difference. That is more logical and lower in risk.

Chapter 2

Taxed to Death — And After: <u>Intergenerational Asset Transfer</u>

— Tim Cestnick, CA —

For most people, death is not a favourite topic of discussion. And as for the topic of income taxes, well, I can think of more than a few other topics that are sure to generate greater excitement. Not to scare you, but this chapter is about both death *and* taxes. Before you skip this chapter for a topic more appealing, let me say that the things we'll be talking about are critical to preserving your wealth. I will be introducing the 10 strategies every Canadian needs to understand when planning for the future. But first, let's look at just why the taxman won't be mourning your death when that time comes.

The Taxman Cometh

It was Ben Franklin who wrote: "Nothing can be said to be certain, except death and taxes." If Ben had been living in modern-day Canada, I'm sure he would agree with one other certainty: death *with* taxes. You see, while Canada does not have a death tax per se, you can bet there are provisions in our tax law that will give the taxman one last dip into your pocket after your death.

When you die, you are deemed to have sold all your capital property. This simply means that, where you've got assets that have appreciated in value, you could end up paying tax on those gains in the year of your death.

Consider James. James died two months ago. At the time of his death, James owned, among other things, a $30,000 Guaranteed Investment Certificate (GIC), a principal residence worth $200,000 that had originally cost him $110,000, and mutual funds worth $100,000 that he had purchased for $40,000 a few years ago. The taxman deems James to have sold, immediately prior to his death, all of these assets at fair market value. The GIC worth $30,000 also had an original cost of $30,000, so there is no taxable gain that results from this deemed disposition. There is a $90,000 gain on the principal residence upon James' death, but he won't face tax on this gain since he can take advantage of his principal residence exemption, which will shelter the gain from tax. As for the mutual funds, the gain of $60,000 will be reported on his final tax return, and he'll have to pay tax on that gain, which will cost his heirs $20,000 in tax at a marginal tax rate of 50 percent.

See how the deemed disposition on death works? There are two points worth noting here. First, cash and near-cash investments such as GICs, term deposits and Canada Savings Bonds will not generally give rise to taxes upon death because these things do not appreciate in value. With no appreciation in value, the deemed disposition rules won't hurt you. Second, your principal residence won't generally face tax upon death because the principal residence exemption typically will offset any gain triggered by the deemed disposition rules.

You should note, however, that where you've got a second property such as a cottage or rental property, you might still face some tax on death since the principal residence exemption applies to one property only. Are there ways to bypass the long arm of Revenue Canada upon your death? Sure there are.

Beating the Taxman Upon Death — And After

Let's take a look at the top ten strategies for minimizing the tax burden that could arise on your death — and after.

1. Leave It to Your Spouse

In the months leading up to our marriage, my wife Carolyn — who was then my fiancée — reminded me on a regular basis that, once married, all that was mine would be hers, and all that was hers would still be hers! Although she didn't realize it, Carolyn hit on a critical element of every good estate plan. You see, there is no easier way to save income taxes than to ensure that all that is yours becomes your spouse's. Upon your death, anything that you leave to your spouse, or to a spousal trust, will avoid the costly effect of the deemed disposition rules.

Let's consider James once again. Table 1 below identifies all James' assets upon his death. Next to the description of the asset is the fair market value of the asset at the time of his death, and his cost (known as the "adjusted cost base") of the asset.

You'll recall that James died two months ago. If he had left all his assets to someone other than his wife — his kids for example — the total income and gains that would be reported on his final tax return would be as described in Table 2.

In this situation, the total taxes paid by James on his final tax return would amount to $342,700 — nearly one-third of his assets. James' heirs would likely use his entire Registered Retirement Savings Plan (RRSP) to pay a portion of the taxes, and they would still be left having to use some of his other investments to pay the balance. Ouch. Now compare the taxes owing if James were to leave everything to his spouse, as shown in Table 3.

Table 1: James' Assets upon Death

	Fair Market Value	Adjusted Cost Base
GIC	$ 30,000	$ 30,000
Mutual Funds	100,000	40,000
Shares of ABC Corp.	25,000	10,000
RRSP	300,000	175,000
Shares in His Own Company	500,000	1
Principal Residence	200,000	110,000
	$ 1,155,000	$ 365,001

Table 2: James' Tax Bill — Kids Inherit Everything

	Gain or Income to Report	Tax Owing
GIC	$ —	$ —
Mutual Funds	60,000	20,000
Shares of ABC Corp.	15,000	5,000
RRSP	300,000	150,000
Shares in His Own Company	499,999	167,000
Principal Residence	—	—
	$ 874,999	$ 342,700

Leaving his assets to his wife would have deferred a full $347,700 in taxes! This tax will eventually be paid by James' wife upon her death, or when she sells the assets. If you're intent on leaving the kids with some of your assets when you're gone, consider giving them the assets that will trigger the lowest tax liability.

Your RRSP and Registered Retirement Income Fund (RRIF) assets should, without question, always transfer to your spouse when possible. If you leave your RRSP or RRIF to anyone else, the full value of the plan will be subject to tax in the year of your death, and you can expect half of that plan to be claimed by the taxman. The only exception is where you have an infirm dependant or a minor child or grandchild who was financially dependent on you at the time of your death. In this case, your RRSP funds can be used to purchase an annuity to age 18 for that child, or transferred to the RRSP of the infirm dependant. You'll still be much better off leaving the RRSP to your spouse, but in the event this can't be done, leaving it to a minor or an infirm person or someone financially dependent on you will at least manage to spread the tax bill over a longer period than otherwise.

Table 3: James' Tax Bill — Spouse Inherits Everything

	Gain or Income to Report	Tax Owing
GIC	$ —	$ —
Mutual Funds	—	—
Shares of ABC Corp.	—	—
RRSP	—	—
Shares in His Own Company	—	—
Principal Residence	—	—
	$ —	$ —

2. Complete an Estate Freeze

An estate freeze is a common technique used to "freeze" the value of an asset today and to pass any future appreciation in value to your kids or another individual. The benefits of doing this are fourfold:

(i)   By freezing the value of an asset today, you'll be able to establish, fairly accurately, what your tax liability will be upon death. This makes planning for your taxes upon death a much easier task.

(ii) By passing the future growth in the asset's value to the next generation you can defer income tax on that growth until a much later time. Taxes may not be due, for example, until your children pass away.

(iii) A freeze may allow you to take advantage of the enhanced capital gains exemption where you own shares of a qualified small business corporation or qualified farm property. This exemption is available to all Canadian residents and can shelter up to $500,000 of capital gains on such property. We now have a $500,000 tax-free rollover on capital gains rolled into a corporation.

(iv) You can enjoy the first three benefits without having to give up control over the assets during your lifetime.

Let's consider our deceased friend James again. James could have completed an estate freeze on the shares of his own business. The shares were worth $500,000 and had a cost of just $1. The freeze could have worked this way: James would have transferred the shares in his own business to a new corporation. In doing so, he could have elected to trigger the $499,999 capital gain accrued on those shares. James could have then used the enhanced capital gains exemption to shelter the full capital gain from tax. In return for transferring the shares, James would have taken back shares in the new company. These new shares would likely have been preferred shares and would not appreciate in value over time (hence the "freeze" is accomplished). Additional shares in the new company would have been issued to James' children. These would be common shares, and all future growth in the business would accrue to these shares.

By the way, our friend James did not complete an estate freeze before his death. Not to worry. He left the shares in his company to his wife, so there was no tax to pay upon his death. Now his wife can complete the freeze and use up her enhanced capital gains exemption and thereby shelter the $499,999 existing gain from tax. Any future appreciation in the value of the business will be taxed in the hands of the children.

3. Negotiate a Death Benefit

What if I told you that you could receive $10,000 of life insurance absolutely free? That's right, no premiums to pay at all. In addition, there will be absolutely no health questions asked or tests administered. In fact, your health is irrelevant. Sounds like a pretty good deal doesn't it? All that's required is your employer's agreement.

You see, our income tax law will allow a death benefit to be paid by your employer to your spouse, child, or anyone else for that matter, completely tax free. It certainly won't make your heirs rich, but $10,000 tax free is worth writing home about, and it's certainly worth a discussion with your employer.

The death benefit must be paid in recognition of your service to the employer. The benefit will be included in the income of the person who receives it, but a deduction of up to $10,000 may be claimed. The $10,000 limit must be shared by any group of people who all received a death benefit in recognition of your service to your employer. And, if the death benefit happens to be paid over more than one year, the total deduction claimed is still limited to $10,000.

Next time your salary level is due to be reviewed, or if you happen to be starting a new position, negotiate with your employer to provide $10,000 tax free to the ones you love.

4. Set up a Testamentary Trust upon Death

You've heard the phrase "the more the merrier." When it comes to paying income taxes, the more people to split the income with, the lower the ultimate tax bill. A testamentary trust is simply another person as far as the taxman is concerned, and adding such a trust to the list of people who will be paying taxes on income from the inheritance you leave behind will save tax dollars. A testamentary trust is a trust created after your death through instructions in your will.

Consider William and Wilma. William died last year and left behind $300,000 in insurance proceeds. He left instructions in his will that a testamentary trust should be created upon his death and that the insurance proceeds should be invested in the trust rather than be paid to his daughter Wilma directly. The result? Tax savings! If the insurance proceeds had been invested in Wilma's hands directly and she had earned, say, $30,000 of interest over the course of one year in addition to her employment income of $60,000, the total tax bill to Wilma would have been $34,500:

Table 4: No Testamentary Trust

	Wilma	Trust	Total
Employment income	$ 60,000	$ —	$ 60,000
Income on inheritance	30,000	—	30,000
Total income	90,000	—	90,000
Taxes owing	$ 34,500	$ —	$ 34,500

Since William directed in his will that a testamentary trust should be created and that the money should be invested in the trust, the total tax bill appears as follows:

Table 5: Testamentary Trust — Splitting Income

	Wilma	Trust	Total
Employment income	$ 60,000	$ —	$ 60,000
Income on inheritance	—	30,000	30,000
Total income	90,000 *60,000*	30,000	90,000
Taxes owing	$ 19,000	$ 8,000	$ 27,000

Notice that when the trust and Wilma share the tax burden, the total tax bill amounts to just $27,000, a full $7,500 less than if Wilma had been taxed on the $30,000 of interest income herself. The reason for this is simple: the first $29,590 — rising to $35,000 as a result of the 2000 budget — of any individual's income is taxed at a lower rate (approximately 23 percent, depending on the province) than dollars over that amount. By arranging to have the $30,000 of interest taxed in a separate individual's hands (the trust's hands) we have arranged for more dollars to be taxed in the lowest tax bracket. If the $30,000 were added to Wilma's income, each of those dollars would have been taxed at approximately 50 percent, depending on the province.

I think it's important to note that when William gave instructions for a trust to be created and for the investments to be made inside the trust, he wasn't robbing Wilma of her inheritance. You see, Wilma was made a trustee (but not the sole trustee) of the trust. The trustees manage the investments on behalf of the beneficiaries. There is only one beneficiary in this case: Wilma. As a result, she can access the investments any time she wants. She can do with the insurance proceeds as she pleases. Whenever the beneficiaries are also the trustees there will be significant control over the assets in the trust.

Finally, you may want to consider setting up a separate testamentary trust for each beneficiary to maximize tax savings. Keep in mind your will must provide that these trusts will be set up once you're gone.

5. Make RRSP Contributions after Death   *To spousal RRSP, spouse must be <69 yrs*

You're probably well acquainted with the benefits of making RRSP contributions. As a refresher, there are two primary benefits: (1) immediate tax savings are available since you'll be entitled to a deduction for any contributions made within your RRSP deduction limits, and (2) you'll enjoy a deferral of tax since the money in your plan will grow without taxation until you decide to withdraw from the RRSP. These benefits don't stop upon your death. Believe it or not, the taxman will allow the executor of your estate to make RRSP contributions on your behalf once you're gone.

Before your executor makes any contributions to an RRSP after your death, there are some basics to understand:

- Once you're gone, no contributions can be made to your own RRSP. Rather, contributions will have to be made to a spousal RRSP. A spousal RRSP is one to which you may make contributions on behalf of your spouse. You'll receive the deduction, but your spouse will pay the tax on any withdrawals.

- Your spouse must be under age 69 on December 31st of the year of your death in order for a contribution to be made to a spousal RRSP. If your spouse is age 69 or over on December 31st of that year, his or her RRSPs will mature and your executor will be unable to make a contribution to a spousal RRSP.

- You must have RRSP deduction room available at the time of your death to enable your executor to make a spousal RRSP contribution on your behalf.

- A contribution to a spousal RRSP after your death will provide a deduction on your final tax return. This can help to minimize the taxes otherwise arising on your death.

The tax savings that will be passed to your heirs from an RRSP contribution after your death will range from 25 percent to 52 percent of the contribution, depending on the level of income on your final tax return, and depending on your province. Generally, where the total income reported on your final tax return is $29,590 or less, the RRSP contribution will save you about $0.23 for each dollar contributed. With an income between $29,590 and $59,180, the taxes saved will amount to about $0.42 for each dollar of contribution. With a taxable income over $59,180, rising to $70,000 over the next five years, your heirs can expect tax savings of about $0.50 on the dollar. Again, these figures will vary slightly by province.

6. Make Charitable Contributions Properly

It seems that in a fit of generosity the government has been making fund-raising easier for charities than ever before. And this would make sense at a time when government hand-outs to charities are thinning out. How are things easier for charities? Canadians are now entitled to make contributions of up to 75 percent of net income to registered charities — and claim a donation credit for it. This figure used to be 20 percent of net income prior to the 1996 federal budget. The 75 percent limit is applied to all registered charities, including gifts to the Crown, and this 75 percent limit is increased to 100 percent of your net income in two situations: (1) in the year of your death and the preceding year, and (2) for donations of ecologically sensitive land and Canadian cultural property.

(a) Gifts of Securities

In addition to these new rules, one other recent change to the charitable giving rules could turn out to be a real windfall for you. You'll benefit from these new rules when you donate securities listed on a prescribed stock exchange to your favourite charity.

Consider our friend James once again. James owned shares in ABC Corporation on the date of his death. ABC is traded on the Toronto Stock Exchange, and the shares were worth $25,000 on the date James died, while he had paid just $10,000 for the shares a couple of years back. These shares were deemed to have been disposed of upon James' death, which would have triggered a $15,000 capital gain, and a tax bill of $5,000 had James not left the shares to charity.

James, however, left instructions in his will for his executor to donate these shares to his favourite charity after his death. The result is that the $15,000 gain is only 33.3 percent taxable! That's right, just $5,000 ($15,000 x 33.3%) of the gain is subject to tax. Normally, three-quarters of the gain would have been taxable under the usual capital gains rules. The result of this preferred treatment is that the tax owing on this $15,000 gain will now be just $2,500 — half of what it would have been. To top it off, a donation credit will be provided based on the $25,000 fair market value of the shares. This credit will be claimed on James' final tax return and will amount to $10,000 (varies slightly by province).

What a bargain James' donation was. Not only did his estate pay less tax on the capital gain on his ABC shares because he left these to charity, but he still received a donation credit. You'll notice that he paid $2,813 in taxes on his capital gain, but received a donation credit of $10,875 to more than offset these taxes. The net benefit to James' estate is $8,062 ($10,875 – $2,813).

Here's how to take advantage of the new rules in your estate planning: where you plan to leave cash to charity after you're gone, consider leaving securities that have appreciated in value instead. This can be done by leaving instructions in your will for your executor to donate specific securities of your choice to a charity of your choice. Your heirs will thank you since the tax savings could be significant.

Here are two other points to consider: (1) The preferential 33.3 percent taxable rate for donated securities applies. Call this an experiment of the federal government if you'd like. (2) You'll be able to take advantage of these new rules during your lifetime as well. That is, donations of securities listed on a prescribed stock exchange during your lifetime will also result in greater tax benefits than prior to the 2000 federal budget.

(b) Charitable Remainder Trusts

Charitable remainder trusts (CRTs) can be a useful tool for your planned giving. CRTs have been more popular in the United States, but are becoming increasingly familiar in Canada.

To understand how CRTs work, consider Jennifer's story. Jennifer has accumulated $75,000 in assets that she would like to leave to charity upon her death. She chose to use a CRT to accomplish this. Here's how it worked: she transferred the $75,000 to a trust with her favourite charity as a beneficiary. Jennifer is also a beneficiary and receives all the income each year that grows on the $75,000 invested inside the trust. Upon Jennifer's death, the charity will receive the "remainder" of the assets inside the trust. Jennifer received a donation receipt in the year she set up the CRT even though she has a right to the income generated on the $75,000 during her lifetime.

There are a few things you need to understand about a CRT before hopping on the bandwagon. First, once you've set up the trust, there's no turning back — it can't be undone. Second, setting up a CRT means giving up control over the assets in the trust, even though you'll be receiving income during your lifetime.

Third, the value of the donation receipt issued to you for setting up the CRT is not simply equal to the assets you've transferred to the trust. In Jennifer's example, she will not receive a donation receipt for the $75,000 transferred to the trust. Rather, the donation receipt is based on an actuarial projection taking into account a number of factors, particularly your age and the expected return on the assets inside the trust.

Fourth, when you transfer assets to a trust, this is considered a "sale" at fair market value, and you could trigger a taxable capital gain. This will be the case when the assets you're transferring have appreciated in value. The tax, if any, may be fully or partially offset by the donation credit, but you'll want to have a tax professional do these calculations for you before setting up a CRT.

(c) Life Insurance

There are a number of ways you'll be able to help your favourite charity through a life insurance policy. Three ways in fact — and each has its own effect on the tax bill your estate will face. We'll look at these in the next strategy — number 7.

7. Use Life Insurance to Fight the Taxman

Life insurance can be an effective tool to reduce your tax burden during your lifetime, and upon your death. Three of the four most common uses of life insurance involve giving money to charity. Before getting to these, let's consider the most common use for life insurance — covering your taxes upon death.

(a) Covering Your Taxes

The deemed disposition rules can leave your estate with a tax bill large enough to wipe out half the assets you were hoping to leave to your heirs. Consider also the result when the second spouse in a family passes away and leaves any remaining RRSP or RRIF assets to the kids: virtually half the assets of the plan will disappear when the taxman comes knocking.

Further, some assets can give rise to a hefty tax bill upon your death without providing the cash for those taxes to be paid. For example, private company shares that have appreciated in value, or a vacation property, can both give rise to taxes, and yet it can be difficult to sell either of these in order to provide the necessary cash to pay the taxes owing.

This is where life insurance can be extremely valuable. If you're able to estimate ahead of time your taxes upon death, you may be able to purchase enough life insurance to cover the taxes owing. Remember our discussion of estate freezes (strategy 2)? A freeze can manage to establish your tax bill ahead of time, allowing for you to purchase the appropriate amount of insurance.

Obviously your age and health will be important considerations in whether this idea is for you. Life insurance may not be an option if you're in poor health or you're elderly. You should note, however, that even where the premiums are high, these may still cost you less than the tax bill upon your death. You may even want to approach your heirs to see if they are able and willing to help cover the cost of these premiums. After all, they are the ones who stand to benefit from a reduced tax burden when you die.

(b) Life Insurance: Charity as Beneficiary

A sure way to help your favourite charity is to name the charity as the beneficiary of an insurance policy on your life.

Consider Joanne. Once Joanne no longer needed the insurance that her policy provided, she decided to change the beneficiary on the policy to her favourite charity. Upon her death, the $50,000 in insurance proceeds were paid directly to the charity. Joanne's heirs benefitted because there were no probate fees to pay on the $50,000 balance since the money never became part of Joanne's estate. Unfortunately, there were no income tax benefits to Joanne's generosity.

Let me repeat that: there were no income tax benefits to Joanne's estate for making the charity the beneficiary of the insurance policy! The rationale offered by Revenue Canada is that the money finding its way to the charity was never really Joanne's since it never found its way to her hands, or her estate's hands. Since it was never hers, her estate is not entitled to a donation credit. This is the taxman's view, despite the fact that Joanne had paid insurance premiums on the policy.

Joanne's intentions were good, and the charity certainly did benefit, but she could have structured her gift to benefit the charity and reduce her taxes upon death at the same time. Let's look at how this could have been accomplished.

(c) Estate as Beneficiary: Donation to Charity

Joanne could have structured her gift differently. Her story could have looked more like this: When Joanne no longer needed the life insurance on her life, she wanted the proceeds of the policy to go to charity upon her death. She changed the beneficiary of the policy to be her estate. Upon her death, the $50,000 of life insurance proceeds was paid to her estate, and she left instructions in her will that $50,000 be left to her favourite charity. When the estate made the contribution, a donation credit was claimed on Joanne's final tax return, reducing the taxes owing by about $22,000.

See the difference? The charity still receives its donation, but Joanne leaves her heirs an extra $22,000 at the same time as a result of the donation credit on her final tax return. The drawback? Probate fees will have to be paid on the $50,000 of insurance proceeds received by the estate. But this is no big deal; the tax savings will far outweigh the probate fees. The only other drawbacks are non-financial, but are worth considering and are as follows: (1)

the gift to the charity could be challenged if someone were to challenge your will, and (2) the donation would be a matter of public record if your will is probated.

(d) Assign or Purchase a Policy

When you simply name the charity as beneficiary, or if you name your estate as beneficiary and designate a gift to the charity in your will, who do you think remains the legal owner of the insurance policy? You do. This next strategy involves transferring legal ownership of the policy to the charity.

Consider Vivek. Vivek had built up enough assets so that he no longer needed the insurance policy on his life which would pay a death benefit of $75,000 upon Vivek's death. He decided to assign the policy to his favourite charity and named the charity as beneficiary under the policy. The cash value of the policy at the time of assigning it to the charity was $30,000. Vivek received a donation receipt from the charity for the $30,000 cash surrender value. This saved him about $13,200 in taxes.

There are a few points worth mentioning here. First, Vivek received a donation credit equal to the cash surrender value of the policy. He won't receive a tax break for the death benefit of $75,000 for the same reasons I introduced in Joanne's situation in (b) above. Second, if Vivek chooses to continue paying the premiums on this insurance policy, he'll receive a donation receipt from the charity for each premium paid. Finally, this assignment of the policy is once-and-for-all. That is, Vivek won't have the right to change his mind later.

Rather than assigning his existing policy to the charity, Vivek could have purchased an entirely new policy on his life for the charity. The charity would own the policy and be named as beneficiary under the policy, but Vivek would make the premium payments. He would receive a donation receipt for each premium paid on the policy. If you choose this option, keep in mind that most charities would prefer policies that build up a cash value and become paid-up (no more premiums are required) at some point in the foreseeable future.

Is it really a good idea to assign or purchase a policy for your favourite charity? It can be. I like the idea best when there's a substantial cash value built up in the policy since you'll get immediate tax relief in the form of a donation credit. If the cash value isn't there, the idea is not as palatable.

Of all three charitable insurance ideas presented here, I prefer (c). That is, I don't think you'll go wrong by naming your estate as the beneficiary under your policy and then providing for a charitable contribution in your will. Doing so will likely provide the most tax relief. On the other hand, you'll receive a donation receipt today, rather than upon your death, if you assign or purchase a policy for the charity. Everyone's situation is different and needs to be looked at individually to determine which idea is best.

8. File More Than One Tax Return

Once you've passed away, your executor is responsible for filing your final tax return. This terminal tax return looks just like the returns you're filing today, except that your final return will cover the period from January 1 (year of your death) through to the date of your death.

Depending on the type of income to be reported on your final tax return, your executor may have the option of filing up to three tax returns in addition to your terminal return.

Consider Harold's situation. Harold died on June 30 last year. Between January 1 and June 30, Harold's income was as follows: $35,000 of salary and $20,000 of interest income from a trust that had been set up on his wife's death. In addition, he was owed the following amounts on the date of his death: $6,000 of vacation pay, $15,000 in commissions, $6,250 in taxable Canadian dividends that had been declared but not yet paid, and $2,000 from matured bond coupons that he had not yet cashed.

Harold's executor didn't realize that more than one tax return could have been used to report these income items — and there are tax benefits to doing this, which we'll see in a minute. As a result, everything was reported on a single terminal tax return, and Harold's estate faced a tax bill as follows:

Table 6: Harold's Taxes — A Terminal Return Only

Income	Terminal Return
Salary	$ 35,000
Trust Interest	20,000
Vacation Pay	6,000
Commissions	15,000
Dividends	6,250
Bond Interest	2,000
	$ 84,250
Taxes Owing	$ 30,280

The fact is, in addition to a terminal return, the option may exist to file up to three more tax returns for the year of death: (i) a rights and things return, (ii) a return for income from a testamentary trust, and (iii) a sole proprietor return.

(i) Rights and Things Return

Rights and things are amounts that were owed to you on the date of your death, and include: dividends declared but not yet paid to you, interest income such as matured bond coupon interest (but not interest on bank deposits), salary, commissions, and vacation pay, among other things. These income items can be reported on a separate tax return to be filed by your executor for the year of your death. We'll see the benefits in a minute.

(ii) Income from a Testamentary Trust

If a family member or friend has passed away and made you a beneficiary of a trust set up by way of their will, you could be receiving income from that trust each year. If you receive income from a testamentary trust in the year of your death, and the trust's year end is not December 31, then that income can be reported on a separate tax return.

(iii) Sole Proprietorship Return

If you happen to be a business owner and operate as a sole proprietorship or a partnership, and your business year end is not December 31st, you'll be able to report certain business income on a separate tax return for the year of your death. Our friend Harold passed away on June 30th last year. If he had owned a business with, say, a January 31 year end, then the business income earned from the date of his last year end (January 31) to the date of his death (June 30) can be reported on a separate tax return.

I should mention that the likelihood of filing a separate tax return for a deceased sole proprietor or partner is not very high anymore. This is due to changes introduced in 1995 that caused many proprietors and partners to change to a December 31 business year end for tax purposes.

Let's see what would've happened if Harold's executor had filed more than one tax return for his year of death. His executor could have filed three different returns for Harold: (1) a terminal return to report the salary Harold had received, (2) a rights and things return to report the vacation pay, commissions, dividends, and bond coupon interest, and (3) a return for the testamentary trust interest income. Here's how things would've changed:

Table 7: Harold's Taxes — Three Tax Returns

Income	Terminal Return	Rights and Things	Trust Income	Total
Salary	$ 35,000	$ —	$ —	
Trust interest	—	—	$ 20,000	
Vacation Pay	—	6,000	—	
Commissions	—	15,000	—	
Dividends	—	6,250	—	
Bond Interest	—	2,000	—	
	$ 35,000	$ 29,250	$ 20,000	
Taxes Owing	$ 8,490	$ 5,150	$ 3,660	$ 17,300

What a difference. The total taxes paid by Harold's estate dropped from $30,280 to $17,300 just by filing more than one tax return! The reason for the savings is simple: each tax return offers a basic personal credit. By filing more than one return, the number of credits is multiplied. In addition, once income is over $29,590 ($35,000 over the next few years) you jump into the second federal tax bracket which will result in a higher tax bill. In Harold's case, we managed to have more dollars taxed in the first tax bracket by dividing the income among more tax returns. The moral of the story is this: the more tax returns filed by your executor, the more money passed to the pockets of your heirs.

9. Minimize U.S. Estate Taxes

While Canada does not levy estate taxes upon death, the U.S. does. If you're a Canadian citizen residing in Canada but you own U.S. property, you could be hit with a U.S. estate tax bill upon your death. Things aren't as bad as they used to be, however. Prior to changes introduced in 1995 in the Canada-U.S. tax treaty, Canadians who owned U.S. assets were subject to U.S. estate taxes on the value of those assets as figured on the date of death. A meagre $60,000 deduction from the value of those assets was provided when making the estate tax calculation. The U.S. estate tax was levied in addition to the taxes paid in Canada, if any, resulting from Canada's deemed disposition rules. The result? Double taxation.

Today, you could still face a tax bill, but greater relief is now provided. Which assets are subject to U.S. estate tax? "U.S. situs property," including real estate (a vacation property, rental property, private home, or business property), shares of a U.S. corporation (public and private companies), debt obligations issued by U.S. residents (individuals or government), and personal property located in the U.S. (cars, boats, jewellery, furnishings, club memberships, and more). The tax is levied on the fair market value of these assets on the date of your death, and the tax rate for U.S. estate taxes ranges from 18 to 55 percent of your U.S. assets, with most people facing a tax bill between 25 and 35 percent of U.S. assets.

Now for the tax breaks offered: Canadian citizens residing outside of the U.S. who have estates of US$1.2 million or less will only be subject to U.S. estate taxes on certain U.S. property. Generally this property will include real estate, business assets when a permanent establishment is maintained in the U.S., and resource properties. In addition, Canadians will be entitled to a unified credit. This credit can be used to offset, dollar for dollar, the U.S. estate tax bill otherwise owing. In actual fact, Canadians won't generally receive the full credit, since it is prorated based on the percentage of total assets located in the United States.

Consider Donna's situation. Donna owned a condominium in Arizona worth US$275,000 on the date of her death. Her total assets upon death were worth US$1,000,000. Donna's U.S. estate taxes were calculated to be US$79,300 before the unified credit. The unified credit that Donna was able to claim was $53,020, calculated as follows: $192,800 x $275,000/$1,000,000. Donna's total estate tax bill was US$26,280 ($79,300 – $53,020). There is a prorated property exemption of US$675,000, rising to $1 million by 2006.

Notice that the unified credit is reduced when only a portion of your assets are located in the U.S., and this will be the case for most Canadians. You'll be glad to know that an additional marital property credit of up to an extra $192,800 is available if you leave your U.S. assets to your spouse upon death. Further, you won't have to worry about the double-taxation problem anymore since any U.S. estate taxes paid will be eligible for a foreign tax credit in Canada (that is, the U.S. estate taxes paid can be used to reduce your Canadian tax bill in the year of death).

You should note that the rules for a U.S. citizen who happens to be living in Canada are slightly different, but if you're in this boat you'll be eligible for similar tax relief.

Let me share with you the top five strategies to reduce the hit of U.S. estate taxes:

(i)   Consider holding your U.S. assets inside a Canadian corporation.

(ii) Gift property to your spouse and children over time since each person is entitled to his or her own unified credit.

(iii) Purchase life insurance to cover any U.S. estate tax liability.

(iv) Restructure your debt so that non-recourse loans are secured by your U.S. assets since this debt will reduce the value of your taxable estate.

(v)   Move your U.S. assets back to Canada.

10. Provide Your Executor with Flexibility

There are a number of strategies that we have talked about to this point. Not all will apply to your situation, but chances are that many will. In order to ensure that your estate is protected from the taxman, it will be important to include in your will any of the strategies here that you want to implement.

At the very least, you should ensure that your will contains a clause that will allow your executor to implement any strategies that he or she considers necessary to minimize taxes on your estate. You may also want to provide in your will that your executor is free to seek the advice of a tax professional before making final decisions on what should be done with certain assets.

Following this advice will ensure that more will be left to your heirs and less to Revenue Canada. And, your executor will appreciate any flexibility you're willing to provide.

CONCLUSION

If there's one person who won't be mourning your death, it's the taxman. As you will have discovered from reading through this chapter, there are some simple ideas that can be implemented to save literally thousands of dollars in tax. It pays to think about the day when you won't be here anymore. Don't hesitate to inform your family ahead of time of what you intend to happen once you're gone, and then be sure to document these intentions in your will. Doing so will avoid any confusion or misunderstanding later, and will ensure that Revenue Canada doesn't get more than its fair share of your estate.

Chapter 3
<u>The Legalities</u>
— Barry Fish, L.L.B., and Les Kotzer, L.L.B. —

Human nature is such that you contemplate controlling your financial affairs from a very personal point of view. True enough, you may retain third parties to assist you with accounting, property management, fund administration, banking, legal matters, brokerage, insurance and innumerable other matters. However, the common denominator to all of these relationships is that they are controlled by you. This chapter contemplates a situation where you are unable to hold these strings of control. Unanticipated events may shift the focus of control away from you. If you die, who will look after your affairs? If you live but you are incapacitated, who will look after your affairs? Inherent in these questions is the risk that third parties who are totally unknown to you may run your empire. Of course, there are answers to these problems, and that is the focus of this chapter.

The chapter is divided into two parts: part one considers the benefits of having a will, which is the after-death situation; part two is devoted to the "living death" situation, whereby you are alive, but for some reason require a third party to look after your financial affairs. This part of the chapter raises the protections of an enduring or continuing power of attorney which survives your incapacity. Note that powers of attorney will never be a replacement for a will and, correspondingly, wills will never be a replacement for powers of attorney. Powers of attorney cannot help after death because death is a terminating event which will extinguish all powers of attorney. Correspondingly, wills can have no effect during life because their triggering event is death.

With this preamble in mind, we will concentrate on the after-death situation to begin with.

PART I: WHY YOU NEED A WILL
For the purposes of this chapter, all references to the third person are intended to be references to both male and female. However, for the purpose of brevity of expression, references to the third person will read "he."

When You Die without a Will
If you do not have a will you will die "intestate." A person who dies intestate has, essentially, been silent as to whom he wants to look after his estate, where his assets will be going, what burial instructions he has and other matters. This silence triggers the operation of provincial legislation. Such provincial legislation will govern who becomes qualified by a court order to take charge of your estate. That person is normally called an "administrator," although in the province of Ontario that person is called an "estate trustee without a will." Provincial legislation will dictate who your beneficiaries will be and the age at which those beneficiaries will inherit.

In essence, without a will:

1. There is no executor in place to act immediately upon your death. Where there is a will, the executor's power exists at the moment of death. However, without a will the administrator's power is suspended until a court order is signed granting such power. Of course, the court order cannot exist and will not exist until a complete court application has been organized, all appropriate consents given, and the court, in its decision, grants such power. This process can take several months.

2. Your children will take their respective shares at the age of majority, as opposed to later ages. With a will, you can suspend the entitlement of a child until that child reaches, for example, the age of 25. With a will you can also stagger the times at which various gifts are paid to your children.

3. An administrator as indicated above must be appointed. However, in order to appoint an administrator, all the beneficiaries must consent. What happens if a beneficiary does not have the capacity to consent? Such a beneficiary may be too young, or may be incompetent. Both of these situations delay the necessary consents, which in turn delays the appointment of an administrator, and of course, during all of this time, the powers of the administrator have not yet started. Accordingly, the estate is "frozen." For example, in the case of the inability to obtain the consent of a child under the age of majority, the matter can be remedied by the person applying to become administrator providing a bond for the estate administration. However, that bond is not free. The applicant must pay premiums to an insurance company to secure that bond. Those premiums will continue until the child reaches the age of majority.

4. Your spouse will not inherit your whole estate. He or she will inherit what is known as the "preferential share" plus a fraction of your remaining estate. The amount of the preferential share and the fraction to which your spouse will be entitled are set forth in Table 1 on page 36.

5. Those who will inherit from your estate are predetermined by a provincial statute. You are governed by a provincial statute that will, in essence, recognise only the fact of marriage and blood lineage and very little else. That being the case, your nephew, whom you have not seen in many years, may inherit from your estate, and your very good friend and your favourite charity will not benefit from your estate. Similarly, because that statute recognises the marital tie, your separated spouse will inherit under the statute because the marital tie has not been broken. Of course, if your separated spouse has validly released his or her right to claim from your estate under a separation agreement, such an agreement will solve this specific problem.

Table 1: Intestacy

Province	Amount of preferential share (after debts paid)	Shares of spouse and one child after preferential share	Shares of spouse and two or more children after preferential share
British Columbia	$65,000	1/2 spouse 1/2 child	1/3 spouse 2/3 children
Alberta	$40,000	1/2 spouse 1/2 child	1/3 spouse 2/3 children
Saskatchewan	$100,000	1/2 spouse 1/2 child	1/3 spouse 2/3 children
Manitoba	$50,000	1/2 spouse 1/2 child	1/2 spouse 1/2 children
Ontario	$200,000	1/2 spouse 1/2 child	1/3 spouse 2/3 children
Quebec	0	1/2 spouse 1/2 child	1/3 spouse 2/3 children
New Brunswick	0	1/2 spouse 1/2 child	1/3 spouse 2/3 children
Prince Edward Island	$50,000	1/2 spouse 1/2 child	1/3 spouse 2/3 children
Nova Scotia	$50,000	1/2 spouse 1/2 child	1/3 spouse 2/3 children
Newfoundland	0	1/2 spouse 1/2 child	1/3 spouse 2/3 children

Remember that all of these problems are eliminated with a will, where you set out the beneficiaries of your choice.

6. You cannot name guardians for your children under the age of majority.

Intestacy

Table 1 sets forth the position in which your spouse and children will find themselves if you die without a will. In order to clearly understand this table, it must be pointed out the term "preferential share" describes a sum of money to which a spouse is entitled before having to divide monies with your children. It is calculated on assets in the name of the deceased after all debts and liabilities have been deducted. Assets in the name of the deceased exclude assets which are jointly owned and exclude assets to which a beneficiary is entitled by contract. An example of such an asset would be a policy of life insurance on the deceased naming a beneficiary under that policy other than the estate. The proceeds of an insurance policy would not be counted as an asset of the deceased, in this example.

References in Table 1 to the shares of the spouse and children are, of course, after calculation of the preferential share. Logically therefore, if the preferential share amounts to $40,000 and the estate amounts to $40,000 the spouse will take the whole estate.

The pattern of decease is never predictable. Without a will, you will be exposing your estate to the whims of fate. It is a common assumption that younger people will outlive the older generation, but consider the following:

1. If you and your spouse are killed in a car accident your children will take your entire estate.
2. If, in addition to you and your spouse, your children also die at the same time or predecease you, the path of your estate depends upon the following:

   (a) If your children themselves left children surviving them, they are known as your "issue." The issue will inherit your entire estate.

   (b) If you and your spouse and your children die leaving no issue, then your estate will be distributed equally between your parents, and if only one of your parents survives you, your estate will be distributed to that parent entirely.

   (c) If you, your spouse and your children die leaving no issue, and you have no surviving parents, your estate will be distributed equally among your surviving brothers and sisters, and if any of your brothers and sisters predecease you, his or her share will be distributed among his or her children equally.

   (d) If you die with no surviving spouse, no children, no issue, no parents, no brother, no sister, no nephew and no niece, your property will be distributed among your next of kin.

   (e) If you have none of the above, the property becomes the property of the Crown (the government).

You can now see the importance of having a will. We will now focus our attention on the will.

Planning for a Will

1. Assets You Cannot Dispose of in a Will

You would think that you could give away everything you own in a will. However, you may not be aware that there are assets that you are accustomed to regarding as your own which in fact you cannot leave in a will because in law they are already spoken for. Consider:

- If you own your house or any other property as a joint tenant with right of survivorship, the joint tenant with whom you own the property will take over complete ownership of it automatically upon your death. The law operates to create this effect wherever there is a joint tenancy with right of survivorship. Accordingly, your will will not be able to pass title on what you do not own at the moment of your death.

- You may own shares in a firm which is subject to a partnership or shareholder's agreement. Under such an agreement, you may not be able to pass title to a partnership interest or to a share unless the partnership or corporation gives approval to such transfer.

- Similarly, a contractual provision in a franchise agreement or in a lease may prevent the passage of the rights to the franchise or the lease in the absence of the consent of the franchisor or the landlord. In a more general sense, a doctor or dentist cannot pass by his or her will the professional rights which he or she has acquired pursuant to the regulatory provisions of the governing associations applicable in the circumstances.

2. Creating a Will Plan

Now that you have a feeling for the type of assets that cannot be disposed of under a will, you can turn your attention to the assets that are capable of distribution under your will. When preparing for your will think of the following:

- If you are leaving property that is encumbered by a lien or a mortgage, who is going to be responsible to pay off that encumbrance? Do you want your general estate to clear the debt so that your beneficiary inherits it debt free? Or, on the other hand, do you want the beneficiary to take the property subject to the lien or mortgage?

- If you have loaned money to someone who will be a beneficiary, do you want to forgive that loan after you die or do you want that beneficiary to owe the money to your estate? In the latter case, is it your wish that the beneficiary have the loan deducted from his or her share of your estate?

- At what age do you wish your beneficiaries to inherit? They cannot take their inheritance if they are younger than the age of majority, but you may wish to delay the inheritance until your beneficiaries become fully mature. Such maturity may not take place at the time of majority, but may in fact occur at the age of 25, 30, etc.

- You need to consider a substitute beneficiary in the event that your primary beneficiary dies before you do. A good example of this is a child who predeceases you. In such circumstances, the substitute beneficiary may be your grandchild or the spouse of that beneficiary.

- Who do you want to serve as your executor? Who do you want to serve as your alternate executor in the event that your first executor is unable or unwilling to act for you?

- Who do you want to serve as the guardian of your infant children?

- You should consider providing for a substitute gift in the event that the gift you intended to leave to your beneficiary no longer exists at the date of your death. For example, if you leave a piano to your brother, what happens if at the date of your death you no longer own the piano? In your will, you may wish to provide that your brother will inherit your stereo if the piano is no longer available to satisfy that bequest.

The Will

It is of paramount importance to be mentally competent at the time that you make your will. The discussion regarding capacity to make a will forms part of this chapter, under the heading "Capacity to Make a Will or Codicil" (p. 49).

When you die with a will, you are dying "testate." A male person who dies leaving a will is known as a "testator" and a female person who dies leaving a will is known as a "testatrix."

The simplest form of will known to law is the holograph will. It is a will completely in your own handwriting and signed by you. There are no witnesses to that will. A holograph will is often used for emergency situations and is not the recommended method of planning your estate. It is not recognised in the provinces of British Columbia and Nova Scotia, except for very limited circumstances. In the rest of Canada the holograph will is recognised, but although recognised it is likely to impose difficulties on your executor when it comes time to prove your will.

A major pitfall awaits those who attempt to do a holograph will by using a stationer's form. The law will not recognise the preprinted portion of a stationer's form if it is used as part of a holograph will. Remember: a holograph will must be *totally* in your own handwriting.

Those who use stationer's forms must follow the formalities imposed by law. The will must be printed or typed and signed by the testator at its end in front of two witnesses, each of whom sign as witnesses in the presence of the testator and in the presence of each other. The will is dated and all pages other than the signing page must be initialled.

Even though it is legal to prepare a will on a stationer's form without a lawyer, it is not advisable to do so. The following are some of the problems that your estate may encounter if you proceed with your will without legal advice:

- Previous wills are not revoked.

- There is no executor appointed and, if appointed, there is no alternate executor appointed.

- The beneficiaries are designated, but the will is silent as to what happens if one of those beneficiaries predeceases you.

- Charities have not been identified properly.

- The language used is too vague to identify a gift.

- The will may contain a clause giving a gift to a beneficiary, but fails to mention what happens if that gift does not exist at the date of your death.

- Your will may not contain adequate powers for your executor and accordingly, he may not be able to fully administer your estate without asking the court for more powers.

PROFESSIONALLY DRAFTED WILLS

The Structure of a Will
In determining the structure of a will, let us deal with the general, then the specific.

General
A professionally drafted will is composed of several parts. For practical purposes we will list them by category, some of which may not require further explanation:

1. identify the testator;

2. revoke any and all prior wills and testamentary dispositions;

3. appoint executors and alternate executors;

4. instruct executors to pay or settle all debts, claims, taxes and duties;

5. grant specific bequests;

6. dispose of residue;

7. provide for guardianship (if necessary);

8. provide administrative provisions including granting of powers, provision for burial and funeral instructions, and survivorship provisions;

9. follow execution format, i.e., dating, signing and witnessing.

1. Identify the Testator

One testator/testatrix, one will. Where a man makes his will he is the testator. Where a woman makes her will, she is the testatrix. For the sake of convenience, we will use the term testator, intending it to apply to both a male and a female, although the proper designation would be testatrix in the case of a female.

Each testator has his own will. The testator has to be identified by his or her proper name. In circumstances of name variation, the phrase "also known as" should be utilized wherever a conservative approach would warrant this precaution. For example, the name "Demetrius" on a birth certificate, where inconsistent with the name "Jim" on a deed or a share certificate, would conservatively warrant the identification of the testator by both names. Similarly, a shortened last name in circumstances of contradiction between birth certificates and naturalization certificates on the one hand, as opposed to legal instrumentation (e.g., deed) on the other, would warrant the same treatment.

Obviously, when preparing to see your lawyer, be sure to have all the variables of your name, all properly spelled, along with the proper names of your beneficiaries.

2. Revoke Any and All Prior Wills and Testamentary Dispositions

Simply put, a clause revoking all former wills, codicils, etc., previously made by you should always be in any new will you are having prepared.

There are no absolutes in life. For instance, although it would be rare, we could envisage a will which contains such a revocation clause, followed by the words "save and except for the provisions of my Last Will and Testament in the State of Florida dated April 5, 1989, the provisions of which I intend to survive the execution of this Will to the extent only that it relates to my property in Florida . . ."

Another concern with respect to such revocation would be, typically, a Quebec marriage contract, which could conceivably contain testamentary provisions. Those testamentary provisions, if conflicting with your intentions, could work considerable mischief if not for this general revocation clause. This comment of course applies more obviously to previous wills. In any event, all is well once the revocation clause is inserted.

3. Appoint Executors and Alternate Executors

In a will, you choose the person(s) who will look after your assets and your affairs after your death. Those persons are defined in law as executors in the plural, or executor for a single male or executrix for a single female. Because the duties imposed upon your executors are to carry out your wishes, it is common for lawyers drafting wills to utilize the term "my trustee" or "my trustees" to designate an executor, an executrix or executors, as the case may be. The term is utilized because for all intents and purposes the duties of an executor coincide with the duties of a trustee in the context of a will. In the province of Ontario, the term "estate trustee" is used to describe an executor named in a will. For the purpose of this discussion, we wish to avoid confusion and you may regard the use of the terms "executor, executors, executrix, trustees and estate trustees," whether singular or plural, as interchangeable. There is no intention to distinguish the one term from the other. For the sake of convenience, we will use the term "executor" for the most part.

Essentially, your executor is the person appointed to make sure that your will is properly carried out. For instance, among other things, your executor is responsible for arranging your burial, proving your will if required, making any claims on behalf of your estate, settling any debts of your estate and satisfying bequests made in your will.

Your executor's power to act comes from his appointment in your will. Obviously, the appointment of an executor in your will is important. Once you die, powers in your will will typically authorize your executor to do almost anything after death that you could do in life. The powers do not depend upon the court grant of probate but rather are in effect instantly upon your death. In the province of Ontario, the probate process is now called "appointment of estate trustee with a will." You might consider the following points when contemplating your choice of executor.

(a) If you are leaving your entire estate outright to your spouse, you may consider the possibility of appointing your spouse as a sole executor, if you feel that your spouse is capable of administering your estate.

(b) One common misconception is that you need more than one executor. If you wish, you can appoint one person as your executor.

(c) Anyone under the age of majority is not permitted to act as an executor.

(d) It may not be advisable to appoint as executor the same person you are considering appointing as guardian of your minor children. Unfolding that matter more particularly, imagine that the guardian has to take your children in and build an extension on his house in times of a recession, severely impairing his own cash flow. Is there justification for a guardian/executor to utilize funds that you have put aside for your children to fund the extension of the guardian's house? This conflict of interest can be avoided by ensuring that the party named as guardian is different from the party named as executor.

If all else fails, remember that there are trust companies who make it their business to fulfil this role of executor. Their involvement is, of course, based upon a fee, but certainly the expense maybe warranted if there is no executor capable of carrying out your wishes.

(e) You should consider whether the person you are appointing as executor has the time to take on the task. An executor may be trustworthy, but he or she may be unwilling to take on the task. Executors have the right to decline the appointment at the outset, when they find out that they have been named. The insertion in your will of a compensation clause for executors would be helpful in ensuring that the executor is paid for his or her trouble. In other words, the executor's compensation clause may prevent your executor from getting "cold feet" on the grounds of his being obliged to sink a lot of time into a situation where his just compensation may not be supported by your will. It is always advisable to obtain your executor's consent before naming him executor.

Tips for Appointing an Executor

- It is advisable to appoint an alternate executor in your will in case your executor of first choice is unable or unwilling to act.

- You may name a relative as your executor even if he is not a beneficiary under your will.

- It is usually advisable to choose an executor who is younger or at least around the same age as yourself.

- If you appoint a "foreign" resident (someone outside of Canada or the Commonwealth) as your executor, he may have to post a bond as security during the course of your estate administration.

- You might consider appointing a trust company in the role of your executor in the following circumstances:
  - if you have no one whom you trust or no one willing and able to act as your executor;
  - if the role of executor would be too difficult in terms of time and effort for your loved ones;
  - if there are trusts set up in your will;
  - if you desire the neutrality offered by a corporate executor;
  - if the managing of the assets in your estate requires specialized skills and expertise;
  - if you anticipate that the administration of your estate will be a lengthy one (for instance in a case where you are setting up a trust for a disabled child).

Appointing a trust company as your executor in these situations will give you peace of mind. A trust company has continuity as opposed to a person who may die or get sick. If you do not wish to appoint a trust company as a sole executor and trustee, you can consider appointing a trust company as a co-executor and co-trustee with a family member.

- If three or more executors are named in your will, you may wish to avoid a requirement for unanimous decisions. To do this, you may consider having a "majority" clause inserted in your will to allow two out of three of the executors to make decisions.

- You can appoint a specialized executor to look after such things as your stamp collection.

4.   Instruct Executors to Pay or Settle All Debts, Claims, Taxes and Duties

Very simply put, the capable executor will pay "just" as opposed to "unjust" or exaggerated debts. Similarly, you will want your executors to take the appropriate tax advice for the purposes of avoiding unnecessary taxes. The typical clause to be inserted in your will should give enough authority to the executor to settle any tax claims just as you would.

5.   Grant Specific Bequests

To summarize, within the will structure, we have so far identified the testator, revoked previous wills and testamentary dispositions, chosen the pattern of executorship, granted authority to pay debts and we are now at that point in the balance sheet of the estate where all of the debts and taxes have been dealt with, leaving us now to deal with the asset side of the balance sheet. The logical approach to the disposition of these assets is firstly to dispose of specific gifts, and then to deal with what is left over, which is called "residue."

When you prepare for a meeting with the professional who does your will, chances are that you will not need to concentrate on specific assets in the circumstances where you expect to be survived by a spouse and children. In this situation, your assets will likely be dealt with generically, usually targeted to your spouse, and if he or she is not alive at your death, then to your children in equal shares.

On the other hand, in the context of a single person with little family to deal with, such as an unmarried person having no parents or siblings, chances are the will instructions will be more heavily asset driven and that specific items will take on a more pronounced importance. For example, you may consider leaving $10,000 to your friend Bill, $15,000 to a specific registered charity, and the residue of the estate to two or three favourite nephews. You should be aware that if you are leaving a gift to a charity, make sure you get the correct name of that charity. If you are leaving a sum of money to a charity and you wish it to be used for a specific purpose, make sure that the purpose is stated in the will.

6.   Dispose of Residue

Many people are so caught up in leaving specific gifts to beneficiaries that they forget to provide for beneficiaries to inherit the residue of their estates. The residue may be distributed immediately upon your death or you may desire your executor to hold the residue for a period of time. You should be aware that there are certain rules (known as "rules against holding in perpetuity") which dictate how long your executor may hold the residue. You should discuss this matter with your lawyer.

If there are a number of people whom you wish to become the residual beneficiaries of your estate, it is usual to divide the residue into shares for distribution among them. If you wish, you may provide that some residual beneficiaries inherit more shares than others, particularly if the estate relates to distribution outside the nuclear family unit.

(a) Unless stated in your will, children will get their inheritance at the age of majority. You cannot provide for payment before that age, but if you wish, you can stagger gifts so that your child or children receive their gifts at various age limits subsequent to their age of majority.

(b) Prior to reaching the age of majority, the child is certainly entitled to the inheritance, but because of age, he or she cannot physically deal with the inheritance and must rely upon the executor/trustee, who takes the inheritance on his or her behalf.

Consider that a teenager, for example, may need money to pay for private school or other needs. In this regard, you can consider having a clause inserted in your will which allows your executor/trustee to hold your child's share in trust with the right to pay out monies from the capital amount (encroachment on capital). You can decide on how wide or narrow the encroachment power should be, but if you do not have any encroachment power, the executor/trustee may not be able to help the child in the time of need beyond the income generated by the capital being held for that child.

(c) You should think about inserting a clause in your will to allow your executor to transfer over what he is holding in trust for minor children, such as a nephew, to the parent or guardian of such minor child. This presumes that the parent or guardian of such child, of course, is not the executor. The absence of this clause may have the unfortunate result of involving the court in the disposition of the monies needed by the child beneficiary prior to his or her age of majority.

(d) Although a child cannot take title to assets before the age of majority, you may want to provide power for your executor to give physical possession of various items that the child considers to be his, such as a TV, radio or bicycle. The clause therefore gives the child continuity of possession.

Residue Tips
- In disposing of the residue of your estate, you should have what is termed a "gift over" (alternate gift) to a person(s) or charity in the event that your residual beneficiary of first preference is not alive at your death. For instance if you are leaving the residue of your estate to your spouse, it is usual that the gift over is to your children in equal shares in the event that your spouse is not alive at your death.

In addition, if you are not married and have no children, and you are leaving the residue of your estate to a friend, you should provide a gift over to another friend, next of kin or charity in the event the beneficiary of first preference is not alive at your death. If your friend was your only named residual beneficiary, and you did not provide for a gift over, the residue would, if he predeceased you, be distributed as if you had no will.

- The residual clause in a will also covers any assets that you acquire after making the will (for example you win a lottery a month after making your will). By having a residual clause, there will always be a beneficiary to inherit assets that you acquire which were not contemplated at the time of making your will.

7. *Provide for Guardianship (If Necessary)*

What if you and your spouse are both killed in a common disaster? Who will take care of your children? Keep in mind that the appointment you make in your will is only effective if there is no other person entitled to custody of the child at the date of your death.

Guardian Tips

- Since the guardian has the right to decline his or her appointment, it is advisable to get someone's approval before appointing him or her as guardian(s).

- Consider the age of the person you are contemplating appointing as guardian(s). A 70-year-old person may find it onerous looking after a 4-year-old child.

- Although the appointment of a guardian in your will is not binding upon the courts (the court will always act in what it considers to be the best interests of the child), your expressed wish as evidenced by the appointment made in your will is an important factor in the formal appointment of a guardian for your children.

- It is a good idea to have an alternate guardian in case the guardian of first choice predeceases you or is unable to fulfil that role.

- Avoid naming the executor as guardian. The reasons for this are referred to above in the discussion regarding executors.

8. *Provide Administrative Provisions, Including Granting of Powers, Burial and Funeral Instructions, and Survivorship Provisions*

It is, as a rule, good policy to give generous powers to your executors so that they can do after your death all that you could do in life, so that your estate can be administered in an efficient manner. Among other powers, some of the powers which would be inserted in your will are the power to sell and convert assets to cash, the power to pay debts, the power to deal with real estate, the power to borrow, the power to deal with interests in companies and the power to divide assets among the beneficiaries without first having to convert them to cash. This is called the power to divide the estate "in specie."

Table 2: Age of Majority

British Columbia	19
Alberta	18
Saskatchewan	18
Manitoba	19
Quebec	18
Ontario	18
Nova Scotia	19
New Brunswick	19
Prince Edward Island	18
Newfoundland	17

Note to Ontario residents: the inclusion of what is commonly known as "the Family Law clause" is an important inclusion in your will. The Ontario law says that the gift you leave your married beneficiary is protected, but unless you expressly state otherwise in your will, the income arising from that gift will be included along with other assets of your married beneficiary and will be subject to division between your married beneficiary and his or her spouse in the event of a matrimonial dispute. If you wish to avoid this situation, you should consider inserting the Family Law clause in your will in order to protect your married beneficiary.

Tips on Executor's Powers

- If you wish to give your executor the power to buy assets from your estate, you should have a clause inserted in your will which empowers your executor to purchase estate assets, if that is your intention. If such a clause is not in the will, the person you have named as executor may have to apply to court for its approval of his or her purchase from your estate. You might consider such a clause if, for instance, you have four children and one of those children is appointed as executor in your will. If that child wishes to buy an asset from your estate such as a cottage, he or she may have to go to court for approval of this purchase unless a specific clause allowing your executor to purchase assets from your estate is included in your will.

- If you wish your executor to have unrestricted investment powers, this should be stated in your will. After your death your executor may have to hold money for infant beneficiaries who may be entitled to those monies when they reach ages such as 18, 21, 25, etc. Your executor will have to invest these monies because of the long period of time involved until such monies can be distributed. There is no question that your executor has the power to invest monies. However, the laws of some provinces restrict your executor to a legislated or regulated list of authorized investments such as government bonds, bank GICs or other conservative investments. If you live in the provinces of British Columbia, Alberta, Saskatchewan, Prince Edward Island or Newfoundland, and you wish your executor to have the power to invest without being bound by such legislated restrictions, as at the time of the writing of this book you must give your executor broader investment powers than what the law provides.

The provinces of New Brunswick and Manitoba have amended their legislation, allowing your executor to invest on a broader basis, provided of course that such investments be prudent. The province of Ontario as of December 1999 has amended the legislation to include mutual funds and most major securities.

- Although most people do not pay much attention to this part of their will, it is a good idea to discuss the executor's powers with the professional drafting your will.

9. Follow Execution Format, i.e., Dating, Signing and Witnessing
The testator, after reviewing the will and thoroughly understanding it, signs it, inserts the date and initials beside the date. He also initials the bottom of every page of the will other than the signing page and any schedule thereto. Similarly, the two witnesses in the presence of the testator and in the presence of each other initial beside the testator and sign their names on the signing page. At this point, the will is fully executed.

You may have heard of individuals attempting to leave their estate by leaving an audiotape or a videotape. Clearly, an audiotape and a videotape do not conform to the formal requirements which underlie the validity of a will. Accordingly, an audiotape is invalid. A videotape is invalid. A will must conform to the above signing and witnessing requirements in order to be valid.

Revising a Will
If money were no object, you would make a new will every time you needed changes, even if those changes were minor. There is nothing preventing you from making a new will, even for minor changes. However, the law does allow a person to make minor changes to his or her will without having to incur the expense of preparing a brand new will. A codicil fulfils this objective.

Many people attempt to make changes to their wills by scratching off words and making insertions with a view to altering the intention set out in their wills. This procedure is very dangerous because the courts may not recognise such alterations. Furthermore, to persuade a court to recognise such alterations would inevitably lead to additional time and expense and might even lead to disputes among beneficiaries and potential beneficiaries. If you want to make changes to your will, it is advisable to follow the long-established recommendations of the legal profession by investing in a brand-new will, or by preparing a codicil.

Capacity to Make a Will or a Codicil

You must be mentally competent at the time that you sign your will or your codicil. Canadian courts have interpreted this phrase to mean that the person making a will or codicil must be of sound and disposing mind at the time such testamentary document is made. If, since the date of your will, you have been subject to declining mental capacity, there is a risk that your codicil may not be effective. For your will or codicil to be valid, you must at the time of signing such will or codicil be capable of understanding what you own and you must fully appreciate where your assets are going. Furthermore, if any force, duress or undue influence is exerted upon you at the time you sign your will or codicil, it may prove to be invalid.

The Codicil

A codicil is a supplement to an existing will which is used when a person who made the will desires to add, change or retract any part of his or her will. A codicil alters certain provisions of your will, adds some new provisions in accordance with your requirements and confirms the remaining provisions of your will. It must be signed with the same formalities as a will. For the purpose of administering your estate, your will will be read together with your codicil or codicils, as if they were one document.

   A codicil, as in the case of a will, can be prepared in holograph form, but for the reasons set forth in the discussion of holograph wills, it is not recommended that a codicil be prepared in holograph form. It is prudent when making a codicil to follow these formalities:

- You must complete the codicil by printing, handwriting or typing the codicil to be signed.
- You must date the codicil.
- You must sign the codicil with your usual signature on the last page, at its

---

A Failed Attempt to Change a Will

The will as typed was prepared validly by a lawyer. All the writing and scratched-out items were done without advice from a lawyer. All the writing and scratched-out items are completely invalid because they failed to follow formalities of the law. People will therefore inherit contrary to the intention of the lady who made the will. The executors who ultimately looked after the estate were not the executors that she tried to appoint.

end, in the presence of two witnesses, who must also sign the codicil in your presence.

- If the codicil is more than one page long, you should initial any prior pages and the witnesses should also initial the prior pages, with all of the initials at the bottom of each page.

- It is also recommended that you and the witnesses insert your initials beside the date.

- It is permissible to have another person sign your will or codicil for you if that person signs it by your direction and in your presence. This will allow a person who is physically challenged to make a will or a codicil. However, the above noted witnessing requirements are still applicable.

The witnessing requirements applicable to a codicil are identical to those applicable to a will. The witnessing requirements have been discussed above.

In order to bring your will and your codicil to probate, if required, the court will have to see an affidavit or a declaration signed by one of your witnesses that he or she saw you sign your will and your codicil, as the case may be, in the presence of himself or herself and in the presence of the other witness. It is therefore going to be very important for your executor to know where to locate the witnesses to your will and the witnesses to your codicil, in order to take steps to probate the will and the codicil. In the province of Ontario, the probate process is known as an application to appoint an estate trustee with a will.

Where to Keep Your Codicil

Your codicil should be kept together with the will that it modifies. Both documents should be kept in a safe place known to your executor, such as a safety deposit box. Remember that both documents will be read as one, so your family should be aware that you have both a will and a codicil.

How to Revoke a Codicil

You may revoke your codicil by destroying it, by revoking it through a new codicil, or by revoking it through a new will. Subject to some technical exceptions, a subsequent marriage will also revoke both your will and your codicil.

PART II: POWER OF ATTORNEY

It is a common misconception that the preparation of your will suffices to complete your estate planning requirements. Declining mental capacity, whether caused by an accident or an illness, may deprive you of your ability to conduct your legal affairs. Your will is completely inadequate to address such circumstances, because a will has no legal effect until you die.

During the time that you are suffering from incapacity, whether of a temporary or permanent nature, you ideally should have the protection of a proper estate plan under which you would appoint a trusted representative to look after both your property and financial affairs through the creation of what is commonly known as an "enduring or encompassing power of attorney." Some provinces have legislation that permits you to create a power of attorney of a different kind, pursuant to which you appoint a trusted person to look after your personal healthcare requirements. One of those provinces is Ontario. The discussion of a healthcare power of attorney is beyond the scope of this book.

Power of Attorney for Property and Financial Affairs

Within this subject, there are yet further divisions which are of critical importance. Although the various types of powers of attorney all bear the same label "power of attorney," there are significant differences between those powers of attorney that will truly protect you from an estate planning point of view, and all other powers of attorney.

Powers of attorney that do not address your needs from an estate planning point of view are exemplified by a bank power of attorney or a power of attorney given for the purpose of granting authority over a specific asset while you are absent. However, the powers of attorney that will serve you in circumstances of your declining capacity, which will properly address your estate planning requirements, are known as "enduring powers of attorney" in some provinces, and as "encompassing, continuing powers of attorney" in the province of Ontario.

What is common to these powers of attorney is the drafting that allows them to survive your subsequent incapacity. That drafting must be articulated in accordance with the specific requirements of each province. For example, wording that will be adequate in the province of British Columbia may not be adequate in the province of Ontario. To further protect you, you should consider signing an enduring or encompassing, continuing power of attorney in those provinces in which you have substantial assets.

Because the forms are specific to each province, and the legislation varies from province to province, we will address this matter on a province-by-province basis. It should be pointed out that in the province of Ontario, the legislation has been changed twice within the last few years, resulting in considerable confusion for that particular province. Accordingly, more in depth treatment is being provided for the province of Ontario.

Province of Ontario

1.   What is a power of attorney for property?

A power of attorney for property is an instrument in writing given by one person (the grantor) to another person or persons (the attorney or attorneys as the case may be) to act on behalf of the grantor in conducting the grantor's financial affairs. In other words, you can appoint someone you trust as your attorney for property who can then sign documents on your behalf relating to your assets and financial affairs.

The power of attorney for property may be general, restricted or continuing depending on your needs. For the purposes of estate planning, the power of attorney we are addressing is commonly known as an "encompassing, continuing power of attorney." It is commonly known as "encompassing" because it covers all of your property, without exception, and "continuing" because it continues past your incapacity. For the purposes of this chapter, such a power of attorney will be referred to as a continuing power of attorney for property.

A continuing power of attorney for property cannot be used to carry out any functions of an office, such as the duties of an executor or a director. Furthermore, a continuing power of attorney for property does not extend to decisions with respect to the personal care or medical treatment of the grantor. For these matters you need a separate and distinct document known as a "power of attorney for personal care." For the purposes of convenience we will refer to a continuing power of attorney for property simply as a CPA.

2.   If you have a will, do you need a continuing power of attorney for property (CPA)?
A CPA and a will are very different documents and serve different purposes. In a CPA you give someone you trust (your attorney) the power to act on your behalf with respect to your financial affairs while you are alive, even if you are unable to act for yourself. The CPA is only operative during your lifetime. After death, the CPA is terminated. At this point, your will takes effect and the executor named in your will has the authority to act. A recent amendment to Ontario law now refers to an executor as an estate trustee.

For the above reasons you should be aware that the executor you appoint in your will has no power to act for you while you are alive. Even if you are legally incapacitated, your executor cannot help you. On the other hand, your attorney appointed through a valid CPA has the power to act on your behalf with respect to your financial affairs while you are alive and unable to act for yourself.

3.   Who can appoint an attorney for property?
If you are over the age of 18 and capable of giving a CPA, you can appoint an attorney for property. Under The Substitute Decisions Act, 1992, as amended by the Advocacy, Consent and Substitute Decisions Statute Law Amendment Act, 1996, a person is capable of giving a CPA if he or she

(a) knows what kind of property he or she has and its approximate value;

(b) is aware of obligations owed to his or her dependents;

(c) knows that the attorney will be able to do on the person's behalf anything in respect of property that the person could do if capable, except make a will, subject to the conditions and restrictions set out in the power of attorney;

(d) knows that the attorney must account for his or her dealings with the person's property;

(e) knows that he or she may, if capable, revoke the continuing power of attorney;

(f) appreciates that unless the attorney manages the property prudently its value may decline;

(g) appreciates the possibility that the attorney could misuse the authority given to him or her.

If you wish to revoke your CPA, you will be able to do so as long as you can meet all of the above tests and, in addition, you comply with the formalities referred to above.

4.   *Who can be appointed as an attorney under CPA?*

You should be aware that the word "attorney" does not mean your lawyer. You can appoint your spouse, your child or anyone else you trust, as long as he or she is at least 18 years of age.

5.   *What are the duties of an attorney?*

Your attorney must exercise his or her powers and duties on your behalf with a very high duty of care. Such a duty is sometimes known as a fiduciary obligation and must be exercised diligently, with honesty, integrity and in good faith, for your benefit. In addition:

(a) your attorney must explain his or her powers and duties to you;

(b) your attorney must encourage you to the greatest extent possible, to participate in decisions about your financial affairs;

(c) your attorney shall promote regular contact between you and supportive family members and friends;

(d) your attorney must consult from time to time with those of your supportive family and friends who are in regular personal contact with you. Your attorney must also consult from time to time with the persons from whom you receive personal care.

Under the provisions of The Substitute Decisions Act, 1992, as amended by the Advocacy, Consent and Substitute Decisions Statute Law Amendment Act, 1996, paragraphs (a) through (d) are based on the assumption that the attorney referred to is acting on your behalf in circumstances where you are not capable.

The Substitute Decisions Act, 1992, as amended by the Advocacy, Consent and Substitute Decisions Statute Law Amendment Act, 1996, obliges your attorney to keep accounts of all transactions involving your financial affairs. In making expenditures on your behalf, your attorney must give the highest priority to expenditures reasonably necessary for your support, education and care. Once that priority is dealt with, the next level of priority is the support, education and care of your dependents. After those two levels of priority, your attorney will then consider your other legal obligations.

6.   *Compensation of an attorney under CPA*

You should be aware that if the attorney who acts for you under a CPA receives compensation, he or she will be expected to exercise the same degree of care, diligence and skill that a professional property manager must exercise. Contrast this with an attorney who acts for you under a CPA where he or she does not accept compensation. In this latter case, your attorney will be expected to exercise the same degree of care, diligence and skill that a person of ordinary prudence would exercise in the conduct of his or her own affairs.

7.   What are the witnessing requirements for a valid CPA?
You must sign your CPA before two witnesses who must sign in the presence of each other. The following persons cannot be your witnesses:

(a) The person you name as your attorney, or his or her spouse or partner. Remember that if a person is your substitute attorney, he or she is just as disqualified as your primary attorney from being one of your witnesses (as is his or her spouse or partner). The Substitute Decisions Act, 1992, as amended by the Advocacy, Consent and Substitute Decisions Statute Law Amendment Act, 1996, defines "spouse" to include a common law relationship where the parties have cohabited for at least one year or are the parents of a child or have entered into a cohabitation agreement under The Family Law Act, 1986. "Partners" is defined by The Substitute Decisions Act, 1992, as amended by the Advocacy, Consent and Substitute Decisions Statute Law Amendment Act, 1996, as two persons who have lived together for at least one year and have a close personal relationship that is of primary importance in the lives of both persons;

(b) your spouse or your partner;

(c) your child or a person whom you have demonstrated a settled intention to treat as your child;

(d) a person whose property is under guardianship or who has a guardian of the person;

(e) a person who is less than 18 years old.

8.   Why is the CPA useful?
The CPA in its unrestricted form gives your attorney the power to do anything you can do with respect to your property and financial affairs with the exception of making your will.

By way of example, the attorney(s) you appoint under your CPA will be able to look after your banking and dealings with other financial institutions even if you are disabled or generally incapable of managing your property. These powers will extend to any other financial or property matters, including the purchase, sale and mortgaging of real estate.

You should be aware that the power of the CPA is effective as soon as it is signed and properly witnessed and the benefits of the CPA will continue even if you become incapable of managing your property. Remember that your CPA is still effective as a regular power of attorney so that if you are away on a business trip, the CPA that you hand over to your trusted loved one will allow that person to manage your financial affairs during your absence. Upon your return, your trusted loved one would hand back the documentation to you for security purposes, if that is your wish.

Although there might not be an immediate need for the attorney, it is common for each of the husband and wife to complete the CPA in favour of the other for use at some later date (for instance, selling or refinancing the family home) in the event of declining capacity, sickness, or unavailability of one of the spouses. Under the law of Ontario, if you are married and own your family's home or condominium, this family home or condominium is referred to as the matrimonial home. In order to sell or refinance the family home, the law requires that both spouses sign the deed or mortgage. This the case even if the family home is in one spouse's name alone. Therefore, if one spouse is incapacitated and has not previously signed a CPA, the able-bodied spouse will not be able to sell or refinance the family home until he or she makes an application to the public guardian and trustee or to the court, as the case may be, for the right to sign documents on behalf of his or her incapacitated spouse. As a result, if you are married and own a family home, it is generally recommended that each spouse should have his or her own CPA.

If you are conducting your estate planning using the CPA which is encompassing over all of your assets, and continuing into your incapacity, such a CPA will have the following benefits:

(a) The power of your CPA does not depend upon an outside event such as the determination of your mental capacity by a medical practitioner or a capacity assessor. The power flows from the instant of delivery of the CPA to your attorney(s). This will prove to be of great assistance to your attorney(s) in his, her or their dealings with your banks and other financial institutions;

(b) Such a CPA will avoid the problems associated with a limited power of attorney because where an attorney has been limited to management of part of the property of an incapable person, it may be necessary for the attorney to agree to a joint management plan with the public guardian and trustee.

If I have a bank power of attorney do I need a CPA?

Many people are under the impression that they are protected in the event of their incapacity by signing a power of attorney at their bank. This is not always the case. The bank power of attorney will only protect you if all of your assets are at that bank. Therefore, if you have other assets in addition to your assets at the bank (for example, your home), you should have a CPA in addition to the bank power of attorney.

In the event that you are using a bank power of attorney in addition to your CPA, your CPA must be carefully drafted so that it will not revoke a prior bank power of attorney. Similarly, if you are about to sign a bank power of attorney, it should be examined so that its wording will not revoke your CPA.

Can I revoke my CPA?

As long as you have mental capacity you may revoke your CPA at any time. The revocation must be in writing and must be signed and dated in front of two witnesses. You will note that the formalities governing the creation of the CPA are the same as the formalities governing its revocation. Once you revoke a CPA, you should notify the financial institutions you are dealing with that your CPA has been revoked.

You should be aware that in addition to revocation, a CPA will be terminated in the following further circumstances:

(a) If the attorney dies, becomes incapable of managing property or resigns in circumstances where another attorney has not been appointed to replace him or her;

(b) if you, the grantor, die;

(c) if you create a new CPA, unless the new CPA provides that there shall be multiple continuing powers of attorney;

(d) if the court appoints a guardian of property.

Does your CPA protect your assets in other provinces?

There is no guarantee that a CPA will be recognised in other provinces. As a result, if you have assets in another province you should consider signing a separate power of attorney in the form recognised by that province.

When can a CPA be acted upon?

A CPA should be carefully drafted to address the point of its commencement. Many people are confused about the commencement of the power. This is a crucial consideration. Where, for example, the power of attorney commences upon your mental incapacity, you may be creating an unintended suspension of the powers of your trusted loved one. If a husband becomes afflicted with multiple sclerosis, or another physical ailment by virtue of which he becomes unable to deal with his financial affairs, his loving wife, whom he trusts, may be barred from utilizing his power of attorney because the wording identified a condition which had to be fulfilled before the power contemplated by the power of attorney would commence. The condition that was mentioned in the power of attorney was "mental incapacity." Multiple sclerosis is a physical ailment, not a mental incapacity.

Caution:

In the past, the Ontario government has distributed free power of attorney forms to the public. Many lawyers have expressed concern about a lay person completing such forms without professional assistance. In fact, the forms themselves caution the lay public to obtain professional assistance before completion of such forms. The instructions on the government form state, "You may wish to have the form reviewed by an expert advisor. If it is not completed properly it may not be valid."

Presumably, by dealing with such government forms, the lay public may trivialize the importance of every word on the document. Trivialization may lead to the following results:

- Unintended revocation of a previously granted power of attorney with respect to a bank or financial institution. What creates this problem lies in the first line of the government of Ontario power of attorney form which states "I revoke any previous continuing power of attorney for property made by me." Banks often use the continuing power of attorney for the purposes of dealing with the affairs of their customers. Such a bank power of attorney, if previously signed is therefore revoked by this clause which appears on the government form.

- The government form raises the possibility of inserting conditions and restrictions on your power of attorney, such as restricting the assets over which your attorney will have jurisdiction. If indeed your power of attorney does contain such a restriction, it is no longer encompassing, and the unintended result will be that your attorney must make an application to the government of Ontario to obtain powers to deal with your property.

- The insertion of a condition pertaining to the commencement of power, as indicated previously above, may create unintended serious delays with respect to the ability of your loving spouse to act on your behalf in the event that you become afflicted with an ailment such as multiple sclerosis.

If you have completed an Ontario government power of attorney form, you should have it reviewed to consider whether the document may protect you.

British Columbia

At the time of publication, the law in British Columbia is governed by The Power of Attorney Act. Under that act, an enduring power of attorney is the estate planning instrument that will allow your trusted representative to act on your behalf in the event of your incapacity. The wording addresses its continuation despite any mental infirmity of the person who makes the power of attorney.

The Representation Agreement Act has received royal assent, but at the time of publication, has not been brought into force, and The Power of Attorney Act continues to apply in the province. If and when the Representation Agreement Act is brought into force, the form contemplated by that act will be known as a representation agreement as opposed to an enduring power of attorney. The following comments address the law as it exists today.

Who can appoint an attorney?
Anyone over 19 and mentally competent can appoint an attorney or be named as an attorney.

What if you did not have an enduring power of attorney and you were to become incapacitated?
Someone would have to apply to a court in order to obtain the power to act for you. That person is appointed under the provisions of The Patients Property Act and is called a "committee." The application to court to appoint a committee requires affidavit materials setting out the assets, liabilities, projected income and living expenses and next of kin of the patient. As set out in The Patients Property Act, doctors must prepare affidavits setting out their diagnosis of the medical condition of the patient and their prognosis for his or her recovery. In the event that the court is disposed to appoint the committee to act on your behalf, it is possible that the committee may have to post a bond as security for his performance. The court may grant the committee more restricted powers than those contained in a power of attorney.

This demonstrates very clearly the importance of having an enduring power of attorney. It avoids the complication and expense of a loved one having to make a court application for the right to act on your behalf in circumstances of your incapacity.

Alberta

The legislation in Alberta governing power of attorney is known as The Powers of Attorney Act of Alberta. Under that act, anyone over 18 and mentally competent can appoint an attorney or be named as an attorney. This legislation allows a person to make an enduring power of attorney, which will allow it to continue notwithstanding the mental incapacity of the donor.

Alberta incorporates two unique formalities into the power of attorney documentation under its legislation:

(a.) The power of attorney form must incorporate the explanatory notes set out in a Schedule to The Powers of Attorney Act of Alberta;

(b) It must be accompanied by a certificate of legal advice signed by a lawyer who is not the attorney or the spouse of the attorney.

What if you did not have an enduring power of attorney and you were to become incapacitated?
Someone would have to apply to a court in order to obtain the power to act for you. That person is appointed under the provisions of Alberta legislation. Such an application would involve considerable evidence and legal expense. In the event that the court would be disposed to grant such powers to a person to act on your behalf, such powers might very well be more restrictive than those contained in an enduring power of attorney.

Saskatchewan

Who can appoint an attorney?

Anyone over 18 and mentally competent can appoint an attorney or be named as an attorney.

When can an enduring power of attorney be acted upon?

The legislation in Saskatchewan governing power of attorney is known as The Powers of Attorney Act of Saskatchewan. Under that act, anyone over 18 and mentally competent can appoint an attorney or be named as an attorney. This legislation allows a person to make an enduring power of attorney, which will allow it to continue notwithstanding the mental incapacity of the donor.

What is its use with respect to real estate?

Saskatchewan has enacted protective legislation known as The Homesteads Act. Under that act, where a spouse owns property, that spouse is able to utilize a power of attorney with respect to real estate dealings, provided that it contains certain clauses which have to be drafted as part of the power of attorney document. However, in circumstances where the husband and the wife live together in a house, and one of the two spouses owns the house and the other does not, you should be aware that there are limitations applicable to the non-owning spouse for his or her protection. The non-owning spouse cannot, by a power of attorney, appoint the owning spouse to act on his or her behalf with respect to the property they are living in.

What if you did not have an enduring power of attorney and you were to become incapacitated?

Someone would have to apply to a court in order to obtain the power to act for you. That person is appointed under the provisions of Saskatchewan legislation and is called a "guardian." The application to court to appoint a guardian may require affidavit material setting out the assets, liabilities, projected income and living expenses and next of kin of the patient. In many cases, doctors must prepare affidavits setting out their diagnosis of the medical condition of the patient and their prognosis for his or her recovery. In the event that the court is disposed to appoint the guardian to act on your behalf, it is possible that the guardian may have to submit an accounting to the court. This demonstrates very clearly the importance of having an enduring power of attorney.

Manitoba

At the time of publication, Bill 59, entitled The Powers of Attorney and Mental Health Amendment Act, has been enacted but is not been proclaimed or brought into force. If and when it is proclaimed, it will have a significant effect upon the power of attorney legislation of Manitoba. The existing legislation is known as The Powers of Attorney Act. This publication is based upon the law as applicable under that act.

Who can appoint an attorney?

Anyone over 19 and mentally competent can appoint an attorney or be named an attorney. If it is your intention to use the power of attorney as an estate planning tool, you must express your intention that your authority will continue after your incapacity. This is known as the enduring clause under the provisions of the above legislation. The power of attorney is known as an enduring power of attorney.

The enduring power of attorney is effective immediately upon being signed and delivered to the attorney to whom it is given. The power comes into force immediately, whether you are capable or incapable of managing your own affairs.

What is its use with respect to real estate?

You should be aware that Manitoba is one of the provinces in Canada that has enacted homestead legislation for the purpose of protecting spouses who are living together or who have previously lived together on a piece of property in Manitoba. One of the protective provisions in the homestead legislation of Manitoba prevents spouses who jointly own real estate from dealing with that real estate if one of the spouses is signing documents on the strength of a power of attorney received from the other owning spouse. A husband must therefore appoint a trusted party other than his wife and of course, a wife should similarly appoint a trusted party other than her husband if what they wish is to protect themselves with an enduring power of attorney which can allow them to deal with property.

What if you did not have an enduring power of attorney and you were to become incapacitated?

Someone would have to apply to a court in order to obtain the power to act for you. That person is appointed under the provisions of Manitoba legislation and, upon being appointed, would be called a "committee." The application to court to appoint a committee requires considerable evidence and can generate considerable legal expense for the proposed Committee. In the event that the court is disposed to appoint a committee to act on your behalf, it is possible that the committee will have accounting obligations. Furthermore, the court may grant the committee more restricted powers than those contained in a power of attorney. This demonstrates very clearly the importance of having an enduring power of attorney.

New Brunswick

Under the provisions of the Property Act, you may grant a power of attorney which will not be revoked by your subsequent mental incompetence. It is known as a durable power of attorney in this province. You have to be 19 in order to name someone or be named in a durable power of attorney.

Without a durable power of attorney, the person to look after you would have to make an application under the Infirm Persons Act. If it is your wish that your power of attorney not be revoked, you should provide language that makes it expressly irrevocable.

Nova Scotia

Under the Powers of Attorney Act of Nova Scotia, it is possible to make an enduring power of attorney. An enduring power of attorney is one that contains a provision expressly stating that it may be exercised during any legal incapacity of the donor. With the appropriate drafting, subsequent legal incapacity will not terminate the authority of the attorney named in the document.

You may draft your enduring power of attorney to include a provision whereby your trusted representative is given the power to preserve and protect your property while you are in a hospital.

Where there is no enduring power of attorney

In the event that you do not have an enduring power of attorney, if you become legally incapacitated, you will have to make an application to the Supreme Court of Nova Scotia for the appointment of a legal guardian. Such an application requires the affidavits of two physicians, two court hearings, a posting of a bond and legal representation.

Who can appoint an attorney?

Anyone over 19 and mentally competent can appoint an attorney or be named an attorney. If it is your intention to use the power of attorney as an estate planning tool, you must express your intention that your authority will continue after your incapacity. This is known as the enduring clause under the provisions of the above legislation. The power of attorney is known as an enduring power of attorney.

The enduring power of attorney is effective immediately upon being signed and delivered to the attorney to whom it is given. The power comes into force immediately, whether you are capable or incapable of managing your own affairs.

Newfoundland

Newfoundland has enacted the Enduring Powers of Attorney Act, pursuant to which you can make an enduring power of attorney. Under that act, you must be 19 years of age in order to name an attorney or to be named as an attorney.

If you sign a power of attorney which is properly witnessed under the legislation and which contains a provision that states that the power of attorney may be exercised during your legal incapacity, that power of attorney will be considered an enduring power of attorney in Newfoundland. The power of attorney must specifically exclude the application of Section 20 of the Mentally Incompetent Persons' Estates Act, in order to exclude government involvement in the management of your estate and in order to exclude a court application.

What if you did not have an enduring power of attorney and you were to become incapacitated?

Someone would have to apply to court in order to obtain power to act for you. That person would be appointed under the provisions of The Mentally Incompetent Persons' Estates Act and is called a "guardian." The application to court to appoint a guardian requires evidence to establish the incompetence and the appointment, if granted, may be subject to the restrictions and duties imposed by the court. This demonstrates very clearly the importance of having an enduring power of attorney.

Prince Edward Island

Anyone over 19 and mentally competent can appoint an attorney or be named an attorney. Under the Powers of Attorney Act, you have the right to prepare an enduring power of attorney provided that your power of attorney contains wording which will enable your power of attorney to be exercised during your subsequent legal incapacity.

What if you did not have an enduring power of attorney and you were to become incapacitated?
Someone would have to apply to a court to obtain the power to act for you.

CONCLUSION

If prior to considering the contents of this chapter you were tempted to trivialize the effectiveness of wills and powers of attorney, or if you were disposed to oversimplify the elements involved in the preparation of these documents, it is hoped this chapter has served to shed some light on the subject. The problems addressed by this chapter are certainly capable of solution, provided that you take reasonable steps to incorporate these documents in your financial planning, as opposed to resorting to them on an emergency, patchwork basis.

Chapter 4

Life Insurance:
The Investment Alternative

— Carmen Da Silva, CA —

Many Canadians fail to realize the growth of their estate is taxable upon their death. It is as though all of the assets are disposed of or sold the moment prior to their death. This "one-time tax" could be larger than all the income tax paid over your lifetime!

No one enjoys paying taxes. It takes a lifetime of hard work, risk and sacrifice to accumulate your wealth. It can be frustrating when taxes and lack of planning threaten the assets that make up your wealth. Remember, the key to estate planning is the orderly transfer of accumulated assets to your intended heirs, with minimum fees and taxes eroding the estate.

If it is worth accumulating assets, isn't it worth researching ways to protect these assets as they pass on to your family or intended heirs? Surprisingly, most people with significant assets overlook the final part of this equation. Many Canadians are not aware that their death may trigger various forms of fees and taxes that can significantly diminish the value of their estate.

Insurance is the foundation of a successful financial plan. During each stage of your life, your need for insurance changes. In the early years you need life insurance protection to replace premature loss of income. As part of retirement planning you need the tax-deferred accumulation available within certain insurance policies. And finally, as part of estate planning, the tax-free insurance proceeds can be used to pay off your estate liabilities.

During your peak working years, your financial planning objectives are focussed on providing an income for your family, reducing your mortgage, educating your children and saving for retirement. Since you have not built sufficient capital, your estate planning goal should focus on income or capital replacement. Life insurance can make up the difference between what you have accumulated and what would be required in the event of disability or premature death. It provides tax-free funds so that your dependents will be able to maintain your desired standard of living, provide for educational needs, pay off the home mortgage, and so on.

Once you have reached retirement years, your financial planning objectives change dramatically. You make the transition from "working for money," to "getting money to work for you." At this stage of your life you want to be reassured that the assets you have worked so hard to accumulate will provide you with the lifestyle you have grown accustomed to.

When planning for retirement income, you must anticipate income from company pension plans and government benefits, then target for assets to make up any shortfall between desired income and income from other sources. At retirement, your accumulated registered and non-registered assets should provide you an income for the rest of your life-time and your spouse's lifetime, if you are married. Proper investment and tax planning will enable you to maximize your after-tax income from these financial resources and support the retirement lifestyle you've always envisioned.

Once your lifestyle needs are met, you should begin to evaluate the long-term impact your investment decisions will have on your estate, in terms of liquidity, taxes and fees. You should research ways to restructure assets or use alternative investments that could have a more favourable impact on your estate. And finally, you should project the estate cost and understand the funding alternatives available to your estate's executor to pay off your estate liabilities.

The previous chapter focussed on taxes triggered by a "deemed disposition" on death, such as income tax on registered retirement savings plan (RRSP) assets and capital gains tax on non-registered assets. This chapter will focus on strategies which utilize life insurance to achieve higher after-tax income and larger estate values.

Part I focuses on the value of tax-exempt life insurance as a powerful tool in your estate and tax planning arsenal. Tax-free insurance proceeds are available to pay the costs that may arise in the estate. This is accomplished by "prepaying" the estate liabilities with less expensive premium dollars. We will also explore ways to get the tax dollars saved, to pay for part or all of the needed life insurance premiums.

Part II focuses on creative strategies that utilize life insurance to achieve higher after-tax income, provide estate liquidity and provide larger estate values by minimizing the impact of taxes and fees.

Part III focuses on the various types of life insurance policies and their characteristics, and illustrates each type of policy.

PART I
Insurance as a Tool to Fund the Estate Settlement Cost

The Projected Estate Cost
As part of the estate planning process you should project the taxes and other liabilities that will result from the "deemed disposition" of your estate assets.

First you should classify assets according to how they will be taxed in the estate. For example,

- registered retirement savings plans (RRSPs) are fully taxable
- the growth on non-registered capital/equity assets are only 66 2/3% taxable
- the growth on your principal residence is tax free.

Next you must take into account various pertinent factors such as the original cost, elected values, current value and projected growth rate of each asset.

Then you must anticipate the depletion of these assets for lifestyle. First, calculate the cash you will require for lifestyle. Subtract this cash need from income you will receive through company or government pensions. This estimates the income you require from accumulated assets.

Once you have projected the growth of the assets and depleted them for your lifestyle, multiply the taxable value of each asset at life expectancy by their respective tax rate. This determines the projected income tax that will result at death. The aggregate tax bill is then added to other fees and expenses, such as probate and legal fees, to give an estimate of the projected estate settlement cost.

In many cases this exposure amounts to more than 40 percent of the total value of the estate, excluding your principal residence.

How to Defer, Reduce and Even Avoid Taxes and Fees

By arranging an orderly transfer of assets to your heir you can reduce, defer and even avoid taxes and fees your estate will incur at death.

For example, you may wish to consider restructuring assets. An "estate freeze" through a holding company can crystallize capital gains tax at their current values, without attracting taxes today. You can also consider incurring a capital gains tax liability today, by gifting or selling assets to your heirs, or transferring assets to a trust.

In both these cases you *defer* capital gains on any subsequent growth to your heirs. Such planning involves complex income tax and non–income tax related issues, therefore such transactions should only be implemented with professionals who specialize in tax and estate planning.

Equity assets within your estate cannot avoid taxation. However, by restructuring the same equity assets within a tax-exempt life insurance you can *avoid* income taxes and probate fees. The income on these assets accumulate tax-sheltered and are paid out tax free upon death. Ultimately you have more assets to use during your lifetime and more assets to pass on to your heirs.

In certain cases taxes cannot be deferred or avoided, especially in the case of an RRSP when the surviving spouse dies. In these circumstances insurance can *reduce* and *avoid* estate shrinkage by providing tax-free funds to pay off the "deemed disposition" taxes at the time of death rather than diminishing the estate portfolio directly. *Estate liquidity* or *estate preservation* through life insurance becomes even more attractive if you can use tax dollars to pay the premiums.

The Alternative Solutions to Funding Estate Liabilities

If you decide to wait until your death and let your estate handle the problem there will be very few alternatives available to your estate's executor.

Your executor could choose to sell the assets that are part of your estate; however, it is often difficult to part with some assets. If there is no liquidity there is usually "liquidation." When death triggers taxes, the executor may be forced to take less than what the assets are worth, especially if the sale must occur quickly or if market conditions are unfavourable.

Your executor could take a loan at the prevailing market rates at the time of your death to cover these liabilities. This may be too high a price to pay for a lack of planning.

If you take matters into your own hands, you can set aside an investment fund. This fund will eventually accumulate an amount that will cover your estate's future liabilities. There are two problems with this method. First, the funds set aside are fully taxable, since the growth will be either taxed annually or on death. Secondly, the fund may be insufficient to cover the costs if you die prematurely.

The perfect answer to your estate problem is a plan that

- you put in place now to avoid unexpected surprises later,

- is tax-sheltered while growing and on death,

- is not affected by prevailing market conditions or rates at death, and

- solves your problem whenever you die.

This ideal solution for funding the estate liabilities is life insurance. With strategic planning, taxes and fees can be deferred until the death of the second spouse. Therefore, if possible, the best type of insurance for estate planning is a joint last to die, term 100 insurance policy (single term to 100 for single individuals). In this way the same death that triggers the tax in the estate also triggers the payout of insurance proceeds, which can be used to fund the tax liability.

Using Tax Dollars to Pay the Life Insurance Premiums

By using life insurance as a tool, you can transfer the risk of funding part or all of the estate liabilities to an insurance company. The cost of paying the premiums over your lifetime can be very inexpensive compared to the alternative of paying the tax from accumulated assets.

Many retirees may find it hard to prepay the estate liabilities in the form of premiums since it affects their current lifestyle. The secret is to use tax dollars to pay for the needed life insurance premiums.

The ability to accumulate income in a tax-deferred investment vehicle gives you the opportunity to use tax dollars saved to pay for all or part of the insurance premiums. Under Section 148 of the Income Tax Act, you are allowed to purchase term insurance for which the annual premiums are funded from a tax-sheltered investment account or side fund. You can enhance estate values, as well as increase retirement assets, through a type of life insurance policy which is often described as a tax-advantaged insurance or universal life insurance.

Within this plan you can deposit relatively large sums of money for the prepayment of the term insurance, subject to certain limits. If the earnings in your account exceed the premium payment, the cost of your life insurance is really paid with pre-tax dollars.

The tax-sheltered side fund can at present be invested in guaranteed investments or you can link your investment returns to mirror the performance of stock or bond indexes such as the TSE, Standard & Poors or Scotia McLeod Bond Index. You can also link your investment returns to mirror the performance of mutual funds such as Trimark, C.I., AGF, Fidelity and Mackenzie. This feature allows the investor to receive competitive fixed income or equity returns on a tax-sheltered basis.

What is in fact happening is that you are creating a separate investment account which, similar to an RRSP, is sheltered until withdrawn, with three notable differences.

- You control the investment mix within competitive investment vehicles (no foreign-content restrictions).

- You determine the amount and timing of any withdrawals (leave the funds sheltered beyond the current age limit of 69).

- You can use the tax-sheltered account as collateral if you do not wish to withdraw the funds and pay the tax.

The added bonus is that, similar to a principal residence, the assets, the tax-sheltered growth and the sum assured all pass on to your beneficiaries tax free. Provided the beneficiary is not the estate, the investment bypasses the estate and moves directly into the hands of the designated beneficiary, thereby avoiding even probate fees.

In conclusion, with proper planning you can fund the tax liability with inexpensive premium dollars by using life insurance. Premiums can be paid, in part or in full, by the taxes saved within a tax-sheltered investment fund. The ability to accumulate income in a tax-deferred investment vehicle means that over time you may earn substantially more than if your money is in a tax-exposed investment, even after taking into account the cost of the insurance premiums. Any taxes saved which were not used for premiums accumulate tax sheltered until withdrawn.

So if you have excess income, from RRIF withdrawals or non-registered assets not required for today's lifestyle needs, this alternative investment strategy not only meets the objective of having tax-sheltered growth to supplement retirement income, but also gives you the ability to transfer assets, tax free, between generations

The tax-deferred investment growth available with "exempt" life insurance policies is not widely known, but is endorsed by tax experts such as Coopers & Lybrand:

> Those looking for tax shelters or deferral mechanisms may wish to explore the benefits that may be derived from an 'exempt' life insurance policy. While professional advice is usually be needed, it is to be noted that a substantial portion of the income from such investments may accumulate free of tax. Such income can also be utilized before death, and the proceeds are not subject generally to tax upon death. If the insurance is surrendered or loses its

"exempt" status, tax may be payable. Assuming this can be avoided, such policies may be a powerful tool in the tax planning arsenal, particularly when virtually all other tax shelters appear to have been curtailed.

—*Tax Planning Checklist 1997-1998*,
Coopers & Lybrand, Chartered Accountants,
(published and © CCH Canada Limited, North York, Ontario)

PART II
Estate Planning: Alternative Investment Strategies to Enhance Retirement Income and Minimize Estate Settlement Cost

Today, retired investors and their advisors are beginning to realize that estate objectives should be a key consideration in long-term investment planning. Investment, retirement, tax and estate planning go hand in hand in long-term financial planning. Since the accumulated assets of retirees are a potential source of further tax revenues, it is critical to structure your affairs to minimize potential fees and taxes at death. As retired investors you should understand the impact your current investment decisions will have on your estate in the event of death.

In addition to investment goals and objectives, your investment strategy should focus on achieving the most desirable results for your estate in the event of your death. Once you are satisfied that your investment will provide you with an adequate retirement income, you should research equivalent investments that provide liquidity, minimize taxes, probate fees and legal expenses upon death. In addition, you may wish to add creditor protection as a key estate objective. By selecting some simple alternative investment strategies it is possible to reduce costs to the estate without having to implement complex structures or expensive techniques.

The life insurance industry has been often overlooked as a source of investment and tax-sheltering opportunities. With the retirement population expanding, many seniors are realizing that there are a variety of strategies that utilize life insurance to achieve higher after-tax income and larger estate values within very flexible plans.

Investing for Income
Many retirees hold a guaranteed investment certificate (GIC) within their non-registered assets. A GIC investment has a guaranteed rate of return, usually with a one- to five-year term of maturity. An alternative investment, equivalent to a GIC but with more favourable results to the estate, is a guaranteed interest annuity (GIA). A GIA investment also has a guaranteed rate of return, usually with a one- to twenty-year term of maturity. Since a GIA is treated as an insurance contract, you can appoint a beneficiary, giving it an estate-planning advantage. Providing the designated beneficiary is not the estate, the investment becomes liquid, bypasses the estate and moves directly into the hands of the designated beneficiary, thereby avoiding probate fees.

Insured Annuity

Today, due to longer life expectancy and relatively low interest rates, many retired investors find it necessary to encroach on capital to meet their lifestyle needs. The risk of outliving retirement assets, or the possibility of significantly eroding the estate, is a considerable strain on seniors.

An alternative investment strategy that can enhance your after-tax retirement income while minimizing fees on death is an insured annuity. A life annuity and a term to 100 life insurance policy are purchased at the same time. The result of this strategy is a lifetime guaranteed income plus guaranteed capital for your estate. Provided the life insurance proceeds are paid directly to a named beneficiary, you can bypass the estate and avoid probate fees. This may be an attractive alternative for retired investors who are looking for guaranteed, regular lifetime income and who want to preserve their capital and avoid the probate and other estate settlement costs.

Table 1: Comparison of Income from a GIC vs Income from an Insured Annuity Strategy

Assume the individual is male, age 75, non-smoker with $100,000 of capital, in a tax bracket of 40%, with an 6% return on a GIC.

	GIC	Insured Annuity
Annual Income	$ 6,000	$ 13,764
Taxable portion	6,000	4,418
Taxes payable	(2,400)	(1,767)
Net After Tax	$ 3,600	$ 11,997
Less: Cost of Insurance		(5,416)
Net Annual Income	$ 3,600	$ 6,581
Annuity Advantage $		$ 3,019

Investing for Growth

During retirement, you may have income or capital in excess of your lifestyle needs. In this situation, it is important to consider the long-term objectives for your excess funds.

When anticipating the depletion of assets for your lifestyle needs, always keep in mind that you should maintain investment in tax-sheltered registered retirement plans for as long as possible. Consider using non-registered sources of capital first. After establishing the proper hierarchy for receiving the required income from your registered and non-registered assets, your attention should then shift to your remaining capital or excess income.

In retirement, surplus income and/or excess capital should be committed to a conservative growth investment strategy — one that is favourable to the estate. The after-tax return on a growth investment strategy should exceed inflation. Maintaining your purchasing power is important because you may need the capital to meet future income needs, for yourself or a surviving spouse.

For many retirees, selecting individual investments and the ongoing management of a growth-oriented investment portfolio may not be desirable. Consequently, the use of equity-based mutual funds has become a popular means of providing a professionally managed, liquid and diversified growth investment strategy.

However, as a senior you should understand the impact an equity-based investment portfolio will have on your estate. For instance, if you were to die at a time when mutual fund units were below your purchase price your estate could face an estate liquidity problem. In addition, the transfer of the units within the estate may be subject to probate fees. Any growth in equity mutual funds triggers capital gains tax upon death, significantly eroding the value of your estate.

If you have excess capital over and above lifestyle needs there is an alternative to investing it in a fully taxable investment. Once again, a tax-exempt life insurance can maximize estate values, as well as provide a source of higher cash flow should you require it. The accumulated tax-sheltered savings from the side fund, as well as the death benefit derived from the term life insurance, are passed on tax free. If the beneficiary is not the estate but rather the heirs directly, one can also bypass the estate and avoid the probate fees. Remember, you have to be insurable to use this strategy; most seniors as they get older may not qualify for health reasons.

Pension Enhancement
Upon retirement many of you will be faced with two or three options for receiving pension benefits from your company or life income fund.

OPTION 1: Single Life Annuity
You can choose to receive maximum pension benefits with no benefits payable to anyone after your death.

OPTION 2: Joint Last to Die Annuity
You can choose a reduced monthly benefit during your lifetime so that your spouse will continue to receive the same monthly benefits if you die first.

OPTION 3: Single Life Annuity with Guarantees
You can choose to receive a monthly amount less than Option 1 but greater than Option 2, of which your spouse will receive 50% if you die first.

Retirement Age 56

	Retiree's Monthly Retirement	Survivor's Benefit
Option 1	$1,667	$0
Option 2	$1,175	$1,175
Option 3	$1,500	$750

The vast majority of couples choose Option 2. By selecting either Option 2 or Option 3 you have essentially purchased a life insurance policy on yourself (that you do not own) which:

- guarantees your spouse a lifetime income,

- may lose its face value but the premium will continue,

- does not permit a beneficiary change,

- does not allow for a contingent beneficiary,

- has no surrender value if your spouse dies first, and

- can never be paid up. You pay for it until death, even if your spouse dies first!

The Solution to This Problem

In order to maximize the value of your benefit (now and after the death of you and your spouse), you may want to consider the following:

Elect Option 1 to receive the maximum pension payment. Use the difference between what you receive and what you would have received if you had chosen either of the other options, to purchase life insurance on yourself. This replaces the lost income to your spouse when you die.

Example:

Monthly benefit	
Retiree selects Option 1	$1,667
Less Option 2 income	$1,175
Savings per month	$ 492
	x 12
Available for Insurance Premiums	$ 5,904

By selecting Option 1, you will receive $492 per month more, which can be used to purchase a life insurance policy to replace the $1,175 income your spouse would have received if you had chosen Option 2 (maximum survivor's benefit).

Will it work? In order to provide a $1,175 monthly income for the surviving spouse, you would need to purchase $150,000 worth of life insurance for $5,904 ($492 difference x 12 months) or less per year. Let's look at the following example:

Available annual savings	$ 5,904
Life Insurance premiums for $150,000 coverage (Male Age 56, Non Smoker)	$ 2,576
Net Increase in Annual income after purchasing life insurance to replace lost income to spouse	**$ 3,328**

Through the use of life insurance to replace the annuity lost on death, you can preserve the capital investment. Upon death a tax-free cash benefit is paid immediately to the beneficiary which eliminates probate and other legal fees.

By using an insurance plan to insure the spouse's income you:

1. pay a lower monthly premium than the pension reduction;
2. purchase a policy whose premiums may end in 10 to 15 years or a lump-sum deposit, resulting in a policy that could be paid up at retirement;
3. have control of survivor benefits;
4. can change the beneficiary;
5. may cash in the policy if your spouse dies first, plus you continue to receive maximum pension benefits;
6. can provide for contingent beneficiaries;
7. may use policy accumulation values to supplement retirement income in later years;
8. accumulate all values in the insurance policy on a tax-deferred basis;
9. can eliminate taxes, probate and legal fees on the transfer of assets, since on death, a tax-free cash benefit can be paid directly to the beneficiaries;
10. provide maximum pension benefits for you and your spouse!

PART III
Various Types of Life Insurance Policies

A life insurance program should be designed to fit your needs at a particular time. Your needs will change over your lifetime. The type of plan, the mortality cost and the features available within any policy should be reviewed periodically. Many people compromise their family's financial security by paying too much for too little coverage.

There are several types of life insurance policies available today. Each type has different features, benefits and costs. The appropriate policy for a specific situation will depend on your present and anticipated future needs.

All life insurance is based on the concept that each individual pays a premium based on the amount of coverage desired. Insurance is priced on a cost per $1,000 of coverage per year. Cost per $1,000 coverage will vary depending on your age, your health and the type of policy purchased.

There are two broad categories of life insurance policies: those that provide only a death benefit, known as "term insurance," and those that provide living benefits in addition to the death benefit, known as "cash value insurance."

Term Insurance
Term insurance generally refers to a life insurance policy which pays out the face value only to the beneficiary upon the death of the life insured. It usually has no cash, savings or investment elements

Types of Term Insurance
Renewable Term (Annual, 5, 10 Year, etc.): The death benefit remains level. Premiums increase at the end of the term, reflecting the increased likelihood of death.

Level Term (Single, Joint Last to Die, Joint First to Die): The death benefit and premiums remain level for a specified period of time, usually to age 65 or to age 100, whenever the death benefit ceases.

Decreasing Term: The death benefit decreases each year even though the premiums remain level. This type of policy is frequently used to cover a mortgage or other loan with a decreasing balance.

Characteristics of Term Insurance
- initial low cost
- increasing premiums over time
- meets specific short-term needs
- has no cash accumulation, or "living benefits"
- finite life

Permanent Insurance
Typically referred to as permanent or traditional cash value life insurance, this type offers guaranteed death benefits, cash values, level premiums and possibly dividends. Cash values are created by the insurance company's investment of excess premiums in a long-term portfolio with legal reserve requirements.

Whole Life

There are several types of cash value life insurance policies to choose from. They are all designed to provide several living benefits as well as the death benefit.

The principal objective of cash value life insurance is the same as term life insurance: to create an immediate estate in the event of the insured's death, and to provide for the needs of their survivors, including the payment of estate taxes. Additionally, the cash build-up inside the policy provides a liquid fund that can be utilized in the event of an emergency or to provide cash, through loans, to take advantage of opportunities that may arise.

Characteristics of Whole Life

- newer policies with lower costs due to upgraded mortality rates
- tax-deferred growth on cash accumulation
- guaranteed cash values supported by company reserves
- guaranteed premiums

Illustration of a Whole Life Insurance Policy

Sex: Male
Age: 35
Class: Nonsmoker

Policy Year	Attained Age	Sum Insured	Premiums	Cash Surrender Value	Paid-Up Values
1	36	100,000	466.00		
2	37	100,000	466.00		
3	38	100,000	466.00		
4	39	100,000	466.00		
5	40	100,000	466.00		
6	41	100,000	466.00		
7	42	100,000	466.00		
8	43	100,000	466.00		
9	44	100,000	466.00		
10	45	100,000	466.00		
15	50	100,000	466.00		
20	55	100,000	466.00	2,420	6.600
25	60	100,000	466.00	3,100	7.080
35	70	100,000	466.00	4,700	8,020
45	80	100,000	466.00	7,120	9,620
55	90	100,000	466.00	10,060	11,760
65	100	100,000	466.00	100,000	100,000

Note:

(1) This illustration assumes that interest rates and insurance charges remain unchanged.

(2) If the interest rates that occur vary from the rates used in this illustration, for any length of time, you may want to change your premium level in order to ensure lifetime insurance protection.

- policy flexibility (may vary premium and death benefit)
- access cash values only through policy loan or surrender
- protection from creditors

Tax-Advantaged Insurance

Universal Life
Universal life insurance was created with flexibility in mind. Within certain limitations, both premium payments and death benefits may be varied to meet the needs of the insured.

This contemporary financial planning product blends two key financial planning priorities — low-cost term insurance and investments — in a single tax-advantaged structure. As you pay premiums, a portion is applied to the cost of term insurance and the balance is deposited into a side fund upon which interest is paid. If the premium paid is not sufficient to cover the cost of term insurance, the shortfall is taken out of the side fund.

You may elect to vary the premiums upward or downward, subject to government maximum limits for sheltering purposes. You may even elect to skip premium payments without losing coverage if there is adequate accumulated value in the cash value portion of the contract.

Characteristics of Universal Life
- lower cost due to updated mortality rates and competitive interest rates
- tax-deferred growth on cash accumulation
- policy flexibility (may vary premium and death benefit)
- access cash values three ways (withdrawal, loan or surrender)
- pass entire cash and accumulated earnings to heirs income tax free
- protection from creditors

Another feature which promotes the concept of the flexibility of universal life is the option to select a managed fund. Unlike traditional life insurance, you may choose the investment vehicle to be used for cash accumulation. The cash accumulation values are dependent upon the return of the chosen investment vehicle.

You select from:
1. a current account, i.e., money market
2. a guaranteed investment certificate (1, 3, 5, 10, 25 years)
3. a bond portfolio
4. an equity portfolio (Canadian, American and international).

Policy holders may change options as their objectives change.

Illustration of a Universal Life Insurance Policy — A (Minimum Premium for Life)

Sex: Male
Age: 35
Coverage: $100,000

Class: Non-Smoker
Face Plus Fund Value Interest Rate: 8%
Guaranteed Cost of Insurance

Year	Age	Total Annual Deposit	Total Death Benefit	Fund Value	Cash Surrender Value	COI Charges	Exempt Line
1	36	509	100,085	85	0	327	2,546
2	37	509	100,177	177	0	327	5,097
3	38	509	100,276	276	0	327	7,652
4	39	509	100,383	383	0	327	10,214
5	40	509	100,499	499	0	327	12,782
6	41	509	100,624	624	0	327	15,358
7	42	509	100,759	759	0	327	17,941
8	43	509	100,905	905	0	327	20,534
9	44	509	101,062	1,062	553	327	23,137
10	45	509	101,232	1,232	1,564	327	25,751
11	46	509	101,416	1,416	1,797	327	28,377
12	47	509	101,614	1,614	2,049	327	31,017
13	48	509	101,829	1,829	2,321	327	33,673
14	49	509	102,060	2,060	2,614	327	36,346
15	50	509	102,310	2,310	2,932	327	39,038
16	51	509	102,580	2,580	3,274	327	41,750
17	52	509	102,872	2,872	3,644	327	44,486
18	53	509	103,186	3,186	4,044	327	47,247
19	54	509	103,527	3,527	4,475	327	50,036
20	55	509	103,894	3,894	4,941	327	52,856
21	56	509	104,290	4,290	5,445	327	54,475
22	57	509	104,719	4,719	5,988	327	56,133
23	58	509	105,272	5,272	6,666	327	57,882
24	59	509	105,880	5,880	7,408	327	59,685
25	60	509	106,548	6,548	8,222	327	61,549
26	61	509	107,283	7,283	9,113	327	63,474
27	62	509	108,090	8,090	10,089	327	65,467
28	63	509	108,976	8,976	11,159	327	67,536
29	64	509	109,951	9,951	12,330	327	69,687
30	65	509	111,021	11,021	13,614	327	71,925
Age	55	509	103,894	3,894	4,941	327	52,856
Age	65	509	111,021	11,021	13,614	327	71,925
Age	75	509	129,676	29,676	35,605	327	102,069
Age	85	509	177,579	77,579	90,712	327	177,579
Age	100	509	421,970	321,970	364,253	327	421,970

Note:
(1) This illustration assumes that interest rates and insurance charges remain unchanged.
(2) If the interest rates that occur vary from the rates used in this illustration, for any length of time, you may want to change your premium level in order to ensure lifetime insurance protection.

Illustration of a Universal Life Insurance Policy — B (Maximum Premium for Ten-Year Period)

Sex: Male   Class: Non-smoker
Age: 35   Face Plus Fund Value Interest Rate: 8%
Coverage: $100,000   Guaranteed Cost of Insurance

Year	Age	Total Annual Deposit	Total Death Benefit	Fund Value	Cash Surrender Value	COI Charges	Exempt Line
1	36	1,500	101,133	1,133	497	327	2,572
2	37	1,500	102,358	2,358	1,086	327	5,208
3	38	1,500	102,358	2,358	1,772	327	7,911
4	39	1,500	105,137	5,137	2,847	327	10,697
5	40	1,500	106,719	6,719	4,429	327	13,573
6	41	1,500	108,538	8,538	6,247	327	16,566
7	42	1,500	110,536	10,536	8,627	327	19,682
8	43	1,500	112,732	12,732	11,459	327	22,941
9	44	1,500	115,145	15,145	14,636	327	26,361
10	45	1,500	117,796	17,796	18,128	327	29,965
11	46	0	119,095	19,095	19,476	327	33,324
12	47	0	120,522	20,522	20,956	327	36,789
13	48	0	122,090	22,090	22,582	327	40,374
14	49	0	123,813	23,813	24,368	327	44,093
15	50	0	125,707	25,707	26,328	327	47,966
16	51	0	127,788	27,788	28,482	327	52,009
17	52	0	130,075	30,075	30,847	327	56,249
18	53	0	132,587	32,587	33,445	327	60,709
19	54	0	135,349	35,349	36,298	327	65,417
20	55	0	138,383	38,383	39,431	327	70,402
21	56	0	141,718	41,718	42,872	327	74,025
22	57	0	145,382	45,382	46,652	327	77,931
23	58	0	149,409	49,409	50,803	327	82,149
24	59	0	153,834	53,834	55,363	327	86,718
25	60	0	158,697	58,697	60,370	327	91,673
26	61	0	164,041	64,041	65,871	327	97,054
27	62	0	169,913	69,913	71,912	327	102,913
28	63	0	176,366	76,366	78,548	327	109,299
29	64	0	183,457	83,457	85,837	327	116,275
30	65	0	191,249	91,249	93,842	327	123,901
Age	55	0	138,383	38,383	39,431	327	70,402
Age	65	0	191,249	91,249	93,842	327	123,901
Age	75	0	327,006	227,006	232,935	327	257,389
Age	85	0	675,000	575,000	588,134	327	675,000
Age	100	0	2,451,626	2,351,626	2,393,910	327	2,451,626

Note:

(1) This illustration assumes that interest rates and insurance charges remain unchanged.

(2) If the interest rates that occur vary from the rates used in this illustration for any length of time, you may want to change your premium level in order to ensure lifetime insurance protection.

Glossary of Insurance Terms

Estate Liquidity — ensuring that your current provisions will provide sufficient liquid assets at death to cover all of your liabilities.

Estate Preservation — keeping the full value of your current estate intact (net of liabilities at death). In order to achieve this, you will have to come up with additional liquid assets at death equal to all of your liabilities.

Guaranteed Interest Annuity (GIA) — basically a life insurance term deposit similar to a GIC. However, a GIA has many additional advantages which make it an estate-friendly investment.

Insured Annuity — an investment strategy whereby a life annuity and a term to 100 life insurance policy are purchased at the same time. This results in a lifetime guaranteed income and guaranteed capital for your estate.

Life Annuity — an annuity which provides a guaranteed income for as long as you live.

Prescribed Annuity — an annuity purchased with a non-registered capital which pays out an equal blend of interest and capital, with only the interest portion being taxable. Because the interest portion is spread out evenly over the payout period of the annuity, this should result in tax savings annually.

Registered Annuity — annuity purchased with a registered source of capital (examples of registered sources include proceeds from an RRP, RRSP, RRIF or LIF). All income is fully taxable.

Term Insurance — generally refers to a life insurance policy which pays out the face value only to the beneficiary upon the death of the life insured. It usually has no cash, savings or investment elements.

Term 100 Insurance — term life insurance policy which has a level cost up to age 100. At age 100 coverage continues with no more premiums being payable.

Universal Life Insurance Policy — in the simplest form, this type of policy provides "term insurance" which is funded through a tax-sheltered investment account or side fund. The side fund can be invested in guaranteed investments, indices or equity mutual funds. At death, the entire proceeds of the side fund and term insurance policy are paid out tax free to a named beneficiary or to your estate.

Chapter 5

Canadians and the U.S. Tax System: How to Minimize Your Exposure

— Kevyn Nightingale, CA, CPA —

As they get older, many Canadians look forward to spending more time in the warm and sunny weather of the southern United States. Some will buy winter residences, and some will even move there.

For other Canadians, the U.S. offers a safe haven against the vicissitudes of the Canadian economic environment. The threat of Quebec separation and our history of tax-and-spend governments make Canada an uncertain place to hold all of your assets.

There are some tax benefits for people entering the U.S. The benefits are biggest for the ones moving there lock, stock and barrel. The benefits are much smaller for investors. But beware — there are traps, too, and they can be painful. This chapter provides a brief list of some of the benefits and costs of entering the U.S.

This chapter discusses cross-border tax issues for Canadian residents who are U.S. "non-resident aliens" (NRAs). An NRA is someone who is neither a U.S. citizen nor a U.S. resident. A "green-card" holder is a U.S. resident for tax purposes, no matter where she actually lives. You can be a resident, even without a green card. U.S. citizens and residents have very special tax issues that cannot be addressed here.

Oh — and a word of warning: don't let the tail wag the dog. If you have a superb income-earning opportunity, the tax implications will rarely turn it into a miserable one. It may make it a little better or worse, but tax implications will hardly ever kill a good deal. The same goes for a change in your lifestyle. It's very easy to get wrapped up in the numbers. Keep in mind that tax is merely one of the decision factors — not the *only* one.

INVESTING AND EARNING INCOME IN THE U.S.

Generally, there is no tax advantage for a Canadian resident investing in the U.S. You'll usually pay the same (or even more) tax on U.S.-source income as you would on Canadian income. If you're going to buy U.S. securities, mutual funds or real estate, do it because you expect to earn better returns, reduce your risk or diversify your portfolio. There are plenty of good reasons to invest in the U.S., but tax is rarely one of them.

Individual Tax Identification Numbers (ITINs)

Since January 1, 1997, every NRA investor in the U.S. has been required to obtain an ITIN from the Internal Revenue Service. When you purchase a U.S. stock or bond, you will be required to give this number to the issuer. When you report income on a U.S. tax return, you will be required to provide this number on the return.

To obtain a number, you must complete form W-7 and send it with proof of your nationality and citizenship to the IRS or a "certifying acceptance agent.[1]" The form is available from the IRS (see the address in the Appendix).

Stocks and Bonds

You may have bought a U.S. stock because you thought it was a better bet than a Canadian one. You may have bought a U.S. bond because you wanted to hold some of your money in U.S. dollars to hedge against a potential drop in the Canadian dollar. Now you have U.S.-source interest or dividend income. How do you pay your tax?

Well, the company that pays you will withhold 10% on interest, or 15% on dividends. (The normal rate is 30%, but the tax treaty reduces the rates for residents of Canada.) So, of your $100[2] of dividends, you only have $85 or $90 in your pocket.

But beware — Revenue Canada will tax you on the full $100 (at rates up to 54%). However, they will give you a "foreign tax credit." The credit is the smaller of:

- the U.S. tax you paid ($10 or $15), and
- the average Canadian and provincial tax on the income

Because Canadian tax rates are so high, the U.S. tax is almost always the smaller figure. What it means is that, in total, you pay the higher of the two countries' tax rates. For cross-border investors, this usually means Canada's.

Canadian versus U.S. Dividends

For dividends, there is one additional tax factor that can be overlooked. Canada has a system of "integration" for corporations that earn income. When you get a dividend from a Canadian company, you get a "dividend tax credit" of 16 ⅔%. This lowers your tax from a top rate of 50% to about 33%.

Dividends from U.S. companies get no such treatment, so when you're investing in U.S. companies, remember to compare the *after-tax* return with your target rate of return. You don't want to earn more before tax just to give it away to the government!

Retirement Income

Normal periodic income from a U.S. pension, 401(k), IRA, Keogh, etc., is subject to a 15% U.S. withholding tax. Lump-sum distributions are subject to regular U.S. tax rates, albeit under some quite complicated averaging rules.

In Canada, U.S. retirement income is taxed essentially the same way as U.S. investment income. The income is fully taxable for Canadian purposes, and you are allowed a foreign tax credit for the U.S. tax paid.

There is one major trap here. When you were working in the U.S. and making contributions to a retirement plan there, you may have been a Canadian resident. You probably got no Canadian deduction for your contribution, and now on the withdrawal, you're going to be taxed again. This situation requires special attention from a cross-border tax professional.

Special Treatment for Individual Retirement Account (IRA) Withdrawals

Generally, it is advisable to leave your U.S. retirement plan intact as long as possible (subject to U.S. limits that force withdrawals, and your need for cash). There is no disadvantage to leaving your money in the plan until you are forced to withdraw it under U.S. law. IRA funds can be invested in a much wider variety of securities, and they don't have the foreign-content limits that Canadian RRSPs have.

You may wish to bring your IRA funds to Canada, and combine them with your Registered Retirement Savings Plan (RRSP). Most of the time it can be done. The IRA withdrawal is taxable, but you get a deduction for the contribution to the RRSP.

The trick is to get a foreign tax credit for the U.S. tax. To do so, you have to ensure that the Canadian tax on your other income is high enough to absorb the U.S. tax. If the IRA is $200,000, and your other income is negligible, you might lose some of the foreign tax credit.

Social Security

Recently, Canada and the U.S. agreed that each recipient would report the income only to the country where she lives. A Canadian-resident recipient of U.S. Social Security reports 85% of the benefit on her Canadian return, and does not report it on any U.S. return. It is not subject to U.S. withholding tax.

REAL ESTATE

Tax Alternatives

Real estate is one of the most popular U.S. investments. Not only can it make money and grow in value, you can visit it or live in it.

There is no treaty protection for investors in U.S. real estate. If you buy U.S. real estate and rent it out, you will be subject to U.S. tax. There are two choices for U.S. taxation:

- you can allow the renter to withhold 30% of the gross revenue,and remit it to the IRS, or
- you can file a return each year, and pay tax on the net income.

It doesn't matter to whom you rent it out; even if the tenant is a Canadian, you must report the income. Some states require returns as well. (Luckily, Florida has no personal income tax.)

The net income route is almost always better. After deducting mortgage interest, property taxes, management fees and depreciation, there is usually little, if any net income in the initial years. Note that depreciation is mandatory in the U.S. (unlike in Canada).

Filing a Return

Usually, the U.S. return is due June 15 each year. If you don't file the return by October 15 of the next year (16 months later) *and* you don't have tax withheld, the IRS can come back and charge you either the 30% or an even higher rate on the gross income. No deductions are allowed.

Many vacation homes are bought for rental as well as personal use. Generally, you are allowed to deduct only the business-use portion of the expenses. If you rent it out for less than 15 days, you don't need to report the rental income or expenses. If you primarily rent it out, and use it personally for less than 15 days or 10% of the days used (whichever is greater), you don't need to consider the personal portion of your expenses. If you file a return and have a loss, the loss is carried forward indefinitely. This can be useful if you sell the property and have a gain.

Calculating the income or loss is so much fun, the IRS makes you do it twice. First, you do a regular calculation, using the regular depreciation rate (27.5 years for residential property, and 39 years for other property). Then you do another calculation, using a lower depreciation rate (40 years). This is for U.S. alternative minimum tax (AMT). Just in case you thought you were finished, you can choose to use the 40-year rate for both calculations.

It's rare for an individual investor to have U.S. AMT, since there's an exemption of $22,500 (if you're married) or $33,750 (if you're not). But the calculation is necessary, since you will likely sell the property, and it matters at that point.

Canadian Tax

Remember, Canada will still tax you on the net rental income. And if you have a reasonable expectation of profit (in the foreseeable future), you can deduct your losses against your other income. If you have to pay any U.S. or state income tax, Revenue Canada will allow a foreign tax credit.

Selling the Property

Withholding Tax

When you sell U.S. real estate, the purchaser will have to withhold 10% of the purchase price and remit it to the U.S. government. This is tax paid on *your* account.

If it's going to be a large burden, you can get the withholding tax reduced by requesting a reduction from the IRS in advance. The IRS will generally allow the withholding tax to be reduced to an amount close to the actual tax you would pay on the gain. You can also eliminate the withholding requirement if the property is going to be used by the purchaser as a personal residence, and the purchase price is less than $300,000.

Reporting the Sale

In any case, you must file a return reporting the gain (or loss). The gain is equal to your proceeds, less your "adjusted basis" and your selling expenses (such as commission). The adjusted basis is the original cost plus the cost of any improvements, less the depreciation taken to date.

Now you know why depreciation is mandatory for income properties. Even if you forgot to claim it on the old returns, you have to reduce the basis as though you had taken it. Of course, if the property was only for personal use and was not rented out, you would not have taken any depreciation.

You also report any rental income or loss. You get to deduct any prior-year accumulated losses on that property. If there's still any income left, you can deduct personal exemptions of $2,800[3] for yourself and each dependent. The remainder is your U.S. taxable income. The gain is subject to tax rates of 10–20% if you've held the property for over one year.

Now for the tricky part. You have to calculate your gain all over again. Remember the Alternative Minimum Tax (AMT) depreciation you calculated each year? You have to recalculate the gain using this depreciation, only this time there are no exemptions available.

Oh, and don't forget about the state. Most states will also tax gains on real estate in their jurisdiction.

EMPLOYMENT

So you're going to work in the U.S. Get ready for a different environment. Most of the locations Canadians go to are just a tad more hard-driving than the ones they come from.

On a *temporary* transfer, the U.S. will tax you on any income you earn, unless:

1. your total U.S.-source income is under $10,000; or

2. you meet all of these tests:

(a) you are physically present in the U.S. under 183 days in the calendar year (this includes personal as well as work time)

(b) you are paid by a non-U.S. company

(c) your employer is not reimbursed for the cost of sending you down by a related U.S. company (this is often a difficult thing to find out).

For example, if your Toronto-based company sends you down for two weeks (10 work days) to work at its affiliate in Miami, and your annual salary is $60,000, your normal year consists of 240 work days, your U.S.-source income will be $2,500 ($60,000 x 10/240), and you will be exempt from U.S. tax under test (1).

Suppose your company wants you to stay there for five months this year. Your U.S.-source income will be $25,000 ($60,000 x 5/12), so test 1 doesn't work. You meet test 2(a) and 2(b). But you have to find out from your employer whether the U.S. affiliate is reimbursing it for your salary to see whether you meet test 2(c).

If you go to the U.S. to work for an affiliate of your Canadian employer, and the plan is to work there for less than five years, you still have to contribute to the Canada Pension Plan. If you didn't work for the Canadian affiliate first, then you will have to pay U.S. Social Security tax. This is one of the few taxes that's higher than the Canadian equivalent.

Usually it's better to pay U.S. Social Security tax, because the tax is eligible for a foreign tax credit in Canada (so your net cost is zero), and the Social Security benefits you will receive in the future are much bigger. Canada has an agreement with the U.S. that allows you to collect a partial pension even if you didn't work there the normal 10-year minimum.

Every state has its own rules as to whether it will tax you. For instance, New York will use your U.S. federal income as the tax base. If you're exempt under the treaty, the base is zero. California does not accept the treaty — if you work there for one day, you're liable for tax. If your main workplace is outside the state, Massachusetts will refrain from taxing you. And some states simply don't tax employment income.

Being exempt from U.S. tax sounds good, but it just avoids some paper-shuffling, and not even all of that. If you're exempt from U.S. tax under the treaty, you still have to file a return to tell the U.S. government that you're exempt.

Remember, as a Canadian resident, you still have to report all of the income you earn in the U.S. on your Canadian tax return. Just as with investment income, Canada will tax you at normal rates, and give you a foreign tax credit for the U.S. and state tax paid.

All this applies only if you remain a Canadian resident. If you're going to move to the U.S. for an indefinite period of time, see "Moving to the U.S." on page 91.

BUSINESS

Are you a consultant? Do you run a business that you're thinking of expanding to the U.S.? Well, the U.S. will tax you on any "U.S.-source" income you earn that is "effectively connected with a U.S. trade or business."

Consulting income is "effectively connected" and "U.S.-source" if the services are rendered by someone physically present in the United States. If your client is American, but you do the work in Canada (by phone, fax or E-mail), you don't have to worry about U.S. tax.

If you ship goods to the U.S., and legal title transfers there, you have income subject to U.S. tax (as well as potential state income and sales tax issues). You may need to review your contracts to see where title transfers.

So here's where the treaty comes in. As a Canadian, you are exempt from U.S. tax as long as you don't have a U.S. permanent establishment (PE). PE includes a place of management, an office, factory and workshop. Generally, full-time employees who are resident in the U.S. constitute a permanent establishment. Right now, Internet web sites that are on U.S. servers don't count as permanent establishments, but look for further developments in this area.

Again, you have to file a U.S. return to report that you are exempt from income tax under the treaty. Canadian residents are not subject to U.S. Social Security tax on business income.

And don't forget about state tax. Each of the 50 states has its own rules about whether your presence is sufficient to create tax. Again, California has the tightest rules.

CANADIAN FOREIGN REPORTING RULES

As you have seen, Canada taxes individuals on their income earned anywhere in the world. In an effort to ensure that all Canadians pay tax on the same basis, the government recently enacted rules requiring Canadians to report their foreign assets.

If the cost amount of the assets totals over $100,000, a Canadian must report all foreign assets[4] except:

- personal use assets (e.g., a Florida condominium that is *not* rented out);
- foreign qualified retirement plans (e.g., IRA);
- assets held by a Canadian registered plan (e.g., an RRSP or RRIF);
- assets used in an active business.

Luckily, this reporting is fairly easy to do. You don't have to disclose each asset — only categories of assets, and ranges of values within each category. There are special rules for offshore trusts and foreign corporations where you own more than 10 percent of the shares.

Penalties for failure to file are severe — $500 per month, up to 24 months. If you fail to file for over 24 months, the penalty is 10 percent of the total cost of the foreign property.

ESTATE AND GIFT TAX

For a Canadian, one of the often unanticipated risks of buying into the U.S. is estate tax. If you die owning certain types of U.S. property, your estate can be subject to tax of up to 55 percent. And this is levied on the gross (fair market) value, unlike the Canadian "death" tax, which is levied only on the gain accrued to the date of death.

Because Canada's tax is on income (the accrued gain), and the U.S.'s is on gross value, they don't mesh very well; it was possible to pay tax of over 80 percent on some assets. Fortunately, Canada and the U.S. signed a protocol to the treaty that provides some relief against double taxation.

Who Is Taxable?

U.S. citizens and residents are taxable on their worldwide estates. As noted above, their issues are too broad for this chapter. Here, we address only non-resident aliens.

Residency for U.S. estate-tax purposes is not quite the same thing as for income tax purposes. For estate-tax purposes, the term "residence" means "domicile." Domicile is the place where you freely choose as the centre of your domestic and legal relations, your principal and permanent residence, with no present intent of leaving. Residence without intention to remain indefinitely does not constitute domicile.

It's hard to change your domicile. There is the presumption that you will continue your original domicile. This presumption can be overcome through a showing of facts and intention pointing to a change. The implication is that people who move to the U.S. can easily become residents for income tax purposes, but may take some time before becoming residents for estate tax purposes. The two concepts are not the same.

What Is Taxable?

In general, a Canadian who has a "gross estate" of $60,000 or more has to file a U.S. estate tax return. The gross estate consists of the following items, which are known as "U.S.-situs" property:

- U.S. real estate (but not mortgages)

- tangible personal property located in the U.S. (e.g., furniture, art, automobiles, but not jewelry and other personal effects of a person who is visiting temporarily)

- assets that are located in the United States and are used in a trade or business

- shares of U.S. corporations (whether publicly traded or not)

- debt instruments of U.S. corporations, individuals and governments (other than cash, bank deposits and debt obligations that pay "portfolio interest." In short, portfolio interest is exempt from U.S. income tax, because the debt instrument is designed to be sold only to non-U.S. persons)

- indirect interests in any of the above held through partnerships. This is a common vehicle for tax shelters and real estate.

The U.S. also has a gift tax (otherwise you could avoid the estate tax by giving property away before your death). For gift-tax purposes, the same property is taxable, except for "intangible" property (most securities). You can make gifts of U.S. intangible property without U.S. gift tax.

The above is a general list. There are other specific inclusions and exclusions too numerous to mention.

Calculation of the Tax

The fair market value of the above items is called the "gross estate." To get the "taxable estate," subtract a portion of

- funeral expenses;
- estate administration fees;
- debts owing by the estate; and
- charitable donations.

The proportion is the ratio of the U.S. gross estate to the worldwide gross estate. So if the decedent's entire estate was a Florida condominium worth $100,000 and a Canadian home worth $300,000, the estate could deduct ¼ ($100,000/$400,000) of the items above.

Sometimes, certain expenses can be deducted in their entirety. For example, if there is a non-recourse debt on U.S. real estate (debt that can only be collected by sale of the property, where the lender cannot demand payment from the owner), the entire debt can be deducted. Charitable bequests can be structured to reduce the estate tax by the entire amount of the donation.

The tentative tax is calculated on a graduated basis, at rates up to 55 percent. A "unified credit" is then allowed covering the first $60,000 or more value, of assets, and a state estate tax credit. Most states have their own estate tax, which is generally calculated as the maximum amount the federal government will allow a credit for.

Canada-U.S. Treaty

As you can see, the U.S. estate tax is quite substantial. At the same time, Canada imposes a tax on the capital gain that has accrued to the date of death. Consider the following examples, calculated using only U.S. domestic law[5]:

- An individual owns only U.S. stocks bought for $400,000 that are now worth $500,000. On his death, they are left to his children. The Canadian capital gains tax is $32,000[6]. The U.S. estate tax is $122,000. If the individual were a U.S. citizen or resident, he would owe nothing.

- The same example as above, except instead of stocks, the individual dies owning U.S. real estate. The tax results are the same.

- The same example as above, except he leaves the estate to his wife, who is not a U.S. citizen. The Canadian tax is zero, as there is no tax on the transfer to a spouse. But the U.S. tax is $143,000. If the wife were a U.S. citizen, there would be no tax. What's more, this problem arises even if both of them lived in the U.S.!

- A well-off Canadian with a diversified portfolio that includes U.S. securities of $2 million, and a total estate of $4 million, dies. She has accrued gains of $500,000. Her Canadian tax is $320,000. Her U.S. estate tax is $743,310 on each of her Canadian and U.S. assets.

As a result of these problems, Canada and the U.S. signed a protocol to the tax treaty that allows the following types of relief:

1. If a decedent's gross worldwide estate is under $1.2 million, the only assets that are subject to U.S. estate tax are real estate[7] and assets used in an active business. The main implication is that most securities are exempt from estate tax.

2. The unified credit will be increased (but never decreased) to the amount determined by the formula:

   Full Unified Credit x (U.S. gross assets/worldwide gross assets).

   This means that individuals with taxable estates under $675,000[8] should not have any U.S. estate tax.

3. On transfers to a spouse, the U.S. will allow an additional "Marital Credit," up to the lesser of:

   (a) the amount necessary to cover the estate tax on the transfer, and

   (b) the treaty-unified credit in (2).

4. Death taxes paid on assets located in one country will be allowed as a foreign tax credit (the tax on the U.S. gains) against death taxes in the other country. In our example, the Canadian tax would be eliminated. The U.S. tax would remain, but that is the price of choosing to invest in U.S. assets. The U.S. tax may be high, but it is not "double tax." Double taxation occurs when the total tax is higher than either country thinks would be proper. It is accepted that cross-border investors will pay the higher of the two taxes.

How to Minimize Estate and Gift Tax

Be careful when you invest. There are no "bad" risks, except for the unknown ones. You can still buy U.S. assets, and avoid or minimize estate and gift tax. Here are a few tips:

- Don't make a gift of U.S.-situs property! If you want to make a gift, make a Canadian gift. Canada has no gift tax.

- The old adage, "the best gift is cash," rings true. There is no U.S. tax on cash. There is no Canadian tax on the deemed gain (as there could be with appreciated property). And there are no reporting requirements.

- When you buy U.S. assets, split the ownership among you and your family by having each member buy a portion of the property. Each individual is entitled to a separate unified credit, and estate tax rates are very steep.

   For example, if one person dies owning a $120,000 condominium, the estate tax can be as much as $16,800. If a husband and wife each have a 50% interest in the same condo, and they both die, leaving their interests to their children, there is no estate tax. Each one's unified credit covers off the $60,000 interest.

- If you already have substantial U.S. assets which you do not want to dispose of to outsiders, you can transfer up to $100,000 per year to your spouse, and up to $10,000 per year to any other person (such as a child). By making regular annual gifts, you can lessen the expected tax bite. But watch for Canadian tax if the property being transferred has gone up in value.

- If you're looking at U.S. real estate strictly as a lifestyle choice and not as an investment, consider renting instead of buying. There is no estate tax on assets you don't own.

- When buying real estate, consider obtaining non-recourse financing for the purchase. Non-recourse debt is fully deductible in calculating the U.S. taxable estate. A non-recourse mortgage is one where the lender is not able to demand payment from you personally should the mortgage have to be paid out and the value of the property is less than the balance owing. For obvious reasons, these mortgages are more difficult to obtain, and more expensive to carry than regular mortgages.

- Many people have used "single-purpose" Canadian corporations to hold their U.S. real estate. The idea behind such a corporation is that it avoids U.S. estate tax (since you don't own U.S. real estate, but only a Canadian corporation). The problem with using a Canadian corporation to hold personal assets is that Revenue Canada believes it could impute a taxable benefit to the shareholders.

  Revenue Canada came up with an administrative solution. If you incorporated a company and met *all* of the following tests, you could avoid the shareholder benefit problem:

  1. The corporation's only objective is the holding of property for the personal use and enjoyment of the shareholder.

  2. The shares of the corporation are held by an individual or an individual and persons (other than a corporation) related to the individual.

  3. The only transactions of the corporation relate to its objective of holding property for the personal use or enjoyment of the shareholder.

  4. The shareholder pays no rent for the use of the property but is charged with all the operating expenses of the property, with the result that the corporation shows no profit or loss with respect to the property on any of its tax returns.

  5. The corporation acquires the property with funds provided by the shareholder or by an arm's length lender, but not by virtue of any interest of the shareholder (or that of a related person) in any other corporation.

6. The property must be acquired by the corporation on a fully taxable basis (that is, without the use of any of the rollover provisions of the Income Tax Act).

7. The corporation may have only one property. The corporation will lose this characterization if it disposes of the property, or if it acquires, even on a temporary basis, more than one property. As a result, a Canadian shareholder who has taken advantage of this policy and who contemplates a change of property would be obliged to incorporate a second corporation.

The concern is that if all these tests are met, the corporation may not have sufficient substance to protect the shareholders from U.S. estate tax. The IRS may "look through" the corporation, and assert that the individuals are the true, beneficial owners.

In addition the corporation, by owning U.S. real property and allowing the owners to use it for personal purposes, could be considered to be renting out U.S. real property, and thus be required to file a U.S. tax return annually. The U.S. has no equivalent to Revenue Canada's administrative position, and there may be U.S. income tax to pay.

An alternative is the use of a "real" corporation that has other activities (such as investment, management or even regular business). As a result of recent court cases, it appears this approach is more likely to be successful.

Where a shareholder causes the corporation to buy a property of specific value to her, the benefit is considered to be the value of the property, multiplied by the statutory interest rate. But if the shareholder makes an interest-free loan to the corporation to fund the purchase, the benefit is offset. If this approach is utilized, it is critical that the shareholder loan to the corporation never be reduced below the amount lent to purchase the property.

Revenue Canada says it may impute a shareholder benefit if the fair rental value of the property exceeds the deemed interest benefit. When the statutory interest rate is low, this risk is one to be considered.

This approach may avoid the Canadian tax problem and the U.S. estate tax issue, but it doesn't necessarily avoid the U.S. income tax problem.

• If you expect that your estate will still be exposed to tax, even considering all of the above items, you can leave your U.S. assets to a Qualified Domestic Trust (QDoT). A QDoT is a U.S. trust that is designed so that withdrawals are subject to estate tax. Some special withdrawals are allowed for medical expenses and such. It doesn't eliminate the tax, but it does defer it until the second spouse dies. (You can't use a Marital Credit under the treaty and a QDoT at the same time.)

• Finally, there is the ultimate option — admit defeat. Prepare to pay the tax.

Depending on your age and health, buy life insurance to cover the liability. Sometimes this is the cheapest option.

MOVING TO THE U.S.

There's no question it's cheaper to live in the U.S. The cost of living in most jurisdictions is lower than in Canada, and the taxes are usually less. So the urge to move can be powerful.

Residency

In general, you are taxed on your worldwide income by the country in which you are resident. Other countries can tax you on income earned there, but rarely can they tax you on income earned in your home country, or a third country.

Residency for tax purposes is easy to establish for most people. They live and work in the same country. But for some people it can be difficult. Snowbirds may say they live in Canada, but spend half the year in each country. Some have homes in both countries, and family in each (or neither). Work may be split, and you may even be married to a national of the other country!

To make matters worse, Canada and the U.S. can't even agree on a common definition of the term:

U.S. Residency

With its highly technical tax system, the U.S. has fairly black and white rules for determining who is a resident. Citizens are taxed on their worldwide income, so residency is not especially important for them. Lawful Permanent Residents ("green-card" holders) are considered resident, no matter where they live (it's not quite as dumb as it sounds).

Substantial Presence

The residency test of interest to most people reading this book is the "substantial presence" test. You are a U.S. resident if the following formula adds up to 183 or more:

- days present in the U.S. in the current year

- days present in the U.S. in the prior year x $1/3$

- days present in the U.S. in the second prior year x $1/6$

The magic number is 122 (about four months). If you are in the U.S. more than four months a year for three years running, you will generally meet this test. So snowbirds are particularly at risk for dual residency.

You must also be physically present in the U.S. 31 days or more in the current year. You can exclude certain days if you are a student, teacher, regular commuter (such as a person who lives in Windsor and works in Detroit), or are there for medical reasons.

Election to Be Resident

In the year you move to the U.S., you may wish to be considered a resident, even if you do not meet the substantial presence test. (Certain deductions and credits are available only to residents.) There is an election available to do so, if you meet the substantial presence test in the next year. There is another election available which allows you to file jointly if your spouse is a U.S. resident.

Closer Connection

If you are remaining a resident of Canada, it's generally inconvenient to be treated as a U.S. resident. There's a lot of tax-filing paperwork, and even potential for significant double taxation. So generally, Canadians will want to be treated as U.S. non-residents.

If you do not wish to be considered a U.S. resident, you can claim a "closer connection" to Canada by establishing that you

- have a tax home in Canada, meaning your principal place of work is in Canada, or if you don't have a principal place of work, your main home is in Canada;

- were physically present in the U.S. fewer than 183 days in the current year;

- have a closer connection to Canada than the U.S. (similar to the Canadian test for residency); and

- file the required form by the tax return due date (usually June 15).

Canadian Residency

For Canadian purposes, residency is determined by where you live, work and play. It is a "facts and circumstances" test that looks at all the factors that could be relevant. Most important are the location of your permanent home, your work, your immediate family, and where you spend most of your time. Of secondary importance are things like bank accounts, club memberships, religious affiliation and community ties.

Once you are a Canadian resident, it's difficult to become a non-resident. To do so, you have to "break your ties" in every substantial manner. Generally, a "clean break" is necessary. You have to move your home, your work and your immediate family (adult children who are not in school don't generally count). You should also close your regular bank accounts, cancel your memberships (or change them to non-resident status), and attempt to sever your major, formal social ties. You should also return your provincial health card, and notify all financial institutions that you will be a non-resident.

Treaty Residency

It's easy to see how you could be a resident of both countries at the same time. For instance, an individual who works in the U.S. but whose spouse and children live in Canada could be a dual resident (assuming she and her spouse are not legally separated).

So there is a risk of double taxation. To simplify the tax planning and compliance, the treaty has some tie-breaker rules to determine residency. A taxpayer is deemed to be a resident of the one country:

1. in which he has a permanent home available;

2. with which his personal and economic relations are closer (centre of vital interests) — this test is similar to Canada's residency test;

3. in which he has an habitual abode;

4. of which he is a citizen.

These tests are applied in order; if one text gives a clear answer, the subsequent tests are ignored. If no test is definitive, the competent authorities of each country are mandated to settle the question by mutual agreement. It is very rare to see the competent authorities settle this question.

If you want to be treated as a U.S. non-resident alien, and are not eligible for the closer-connection exception, you can often use the treaty to get the same result. But you have to file a disclosure with the IRS to indicate that you're doing so, or else face a penalty. Canada has no such requirement — yet.

U.S. Taxable Income

Everybody knows the U.S. tax rates are lower than the Canadian ones. But even more important is the fact that the base they are levied on is usually smaller than the Canadian one.

Most important, a married couple can file jointly. In Canada, spouses must file separately. If one spouse is a much higher earner, she gets whacked with super-high tax rates; the other pays very little. In total they pay more than a family with two separate incomes of similar size. For example, a family with two spouses, each earning CAN$30,000,[9] pays $8,901 in income tax. The same family, where one spouse makes $60,000 and the other stays at home, pays $16,311.[10] That's why income-splitting is a favoured Canadian tax-minimization technique. In the U.S., because there is joint filing, the "averaging" effect accomplishes the goal of income splitting. If the families were in the U.S., there would be no difference in their tax liabilities.

In calculating U.S. taxable income, you get to deduct mortgage interest, property taxes and medical expenses.[11] For most people, the first two are fairly big items. And if you don't have much in the way of these items, you can take a "standard deduction." This deduction is $7,350 for a married couple. It is $800 more for each spouse who is 65 or older. And then there are exemptions of $2,800 per person in the family.[12]

These deductions and exemptions all reduce tax at the taxpayer's highest marginal rate. Contrast this with Canada's personal credits, which (aside from the one for charitable donations), only reduce tax at the lowest rate.

The U.S. does not have RRSPs, but they do have pension plans, 401(k) plans,

Keogh plans, self-employed plans, and Individual Retirement Arrangements (IRA) that function in a similar manner.

On the other hand, there are some drawbacks: The U.S. taxes gambling winnings. If you intend to own a Canadian corporation or trust after becoming a U.S. resident, you will help keep the paper companies in business — U.S. tax law is very suspicious of foreign corporations, and there are major reporting obligations for U.S. individuals in these positions. There can also be double taxation of income.

The U.S. also taxes gains on your principal residence. However, if you keep "buying up," you can defer the tax until you cash out. And if you're over age 55, you can take a one-time exclusion of $125,000. There's even talk in Congress about increasing it to $500,000.

STRATEGIES FOR EMIGRATION FROM CANADA

How to File Your Final Canadian Return
When you leave, you will report on your Canadian return

- worldwide income to the date of departure,

- gains on assets owned at the time of departure, and

- certain Canadian-source income subsequent to departure. This will not include income that is subject only to a flat withholding tax, but it will include employment and business income earned in Canada.

Income earned after the departure date and subject to withholding tax, such as interest, dividends and royalties, does not appear on the return. The payers need to be informed so they can withhold the appropriate tax.

Rental Income
If you rent out your Canadian home, or retain a Canadian rental property after emigrating, you have a choice similar to the one discussed above for Canadians owing U.S. rental property. You may

1. allow the tenant to remit 25 percent of the gross revenue to Revenue Canada on a monthly basis, or

2. notify Revenue Canada that you plan to file a return each year by June 30. In this case, the tenant needs only to remit 25 percent of the anticipated net income, before capital cost allowance (CCA is tax depreciation), to Revenue Canada on a monthly basis.

If you choose #1, you need do nothing further. If you choose #2, you must file a return.

Filing a Return for Rental Income

You can (or with option #2, must) file an annual tax return reporting just this income (or loss). You can claim CCA on this return. The general rate is 4 percent per year, with 2 percent allowed in the first year. CCA cannot create or increase your total rental loss.

As with the U.S. choice, option #2 is usually the best, since the net income is generally a small number, compared with the gross revenue.

In case you chose option #1, maybe by default, and didn't notify Revenue Canada that you were going to file a return, you have two years to file a return and get a refund for any overpaid tax. Revenue Canada will not usually allow filing of a return beyond the two-year period.

Canadian "Exit" Tax

Canada has a "closed" tax system. If, at the time you leave Canada (become a non-resident), you owned assets that were worth more than the price you paid for them, you will have a "deemed disposition." You will be treated as having sold the assets to yourself for fair market value. The gain is then included on your final tax return. This applies to all assets where the value has increased, not just capital assets. There are some exceptions:

1. Canadian real estate. Canada ensures that tax is paid upon ultimate disposal by having the eventual purchaser withhold Canadian tax. You then have to file a return to get any refund. In fact, the required withholding of 30 percent of the proceeds usually far exceeds the gain, so prior to sale, it is usually appropriate to ask Revenue Canada for permission to reduce the withholding.

2. assets used in an active business;

3. interest in a partnership where the assets are used in an active business;

4. interests in deferred income plans (RRSPs, pension plans, etc.). Payments out of these are subject to non-resident withholding tax by the plan administrator.

Note that the list no longer includes shares of private Canadian corporations, or of large blocks of public corporations. Effective October 1, 1996, these assets are not eligible for automatic deferral.

You may have "winners" (where there are accrued gains) and "losers" (with accrued losses). If the sum of the losers exceeds the winners, the net loss cannot be claimed.

It is possible to elect to defer payment of tax until the time of actual disposition. However, the election must be filed before the due date of the return, and "adequate security" must be filed with the minister.

In the past, the minister would only accept "hard" security — government bonds, blue-chip securities, or real estate. However, with the 1996 changes, it may be difficult or impossible to provide this type of security. Revenue Canada has said it would consider accepting the shares of the corporation itself as security, provided the value of the shares was unlikely to be impaired (not always something that can be guaranteed in this world). We have yet to see how this law will play out in real life.

Conflict with U.S. Capital Gains Tax System

Unlike Canada and Australia, the U.S. doesn't recognize deemed gains upon moving. If you own an asset in Canada, move to the U.S. and then sell it, you'll usually have to pay U.S. tax on the full gain, based on the actual, original cost to you. This is the taxation, notwithstanding the fact that you already paid Canadian tax on the deemed disposition on emigration. It can make for a pretty ugly tax year, since the foreign tax credits may not fully offset the double taxation. Sometimes it's better to actually sell some of your appreciated property before moving.

This scenario is not usually a problem for Canadian real estate, business assets or deferred income plans (RRSPs, etc.), since Canada doesn't deem a disposition of them when you leave (and under the treaty, the U.S. will recognize an increased basis for your principal residence). But for other assets, particularly shares of private corporations, some strategies need to be employed in order to avoid double taxation. These strategies are beyond the scope of this book.

Receipt of Income from Canadian Registered Plans While a U.S. Resident

Canadian Taxation

Canadian pension plans, RRSPs and RRIFs provide a special benefit for Canadians moving to the U.S. Firstly, the original contribution was deductible, providing a tax benefit of up to 54 percent. Secondly, the income earned in the plan has been exempt from tax to date. Thirdly, withdrawals from the plan as a non-resident are subject only to non-resident tax of 25 percent. This tax is reduced on periodic payments to 15 percent.

There is an election available to file a regular return, reporting Canadian retiring allowances, pension-type payments, CPP, QPP and OAS (called "Canadian benefits"). This election can be beneficial if these payments constitute 50 percent or more of your worldwide net income and your worldwide income is low. In essence, you have to complete a Canadian tax return as though you are resident (reporting worldwide income), and determine an average tax rate on your income. This average tax rate will then be applied to the "Canadian benefits." For low- and moderate-income individuals, this rate can be lower than the withholding tax rate of 15–25 percent.

U.S. Taxation

Usually there is no U.S. tax on a RRSP or RRIF withdrawal. One reason is that the "income" for U.S. purposes is generally much less than for Canadian purposes. The U.S. views an RRSP as just a regular securities account. Gains and losses are accorded no special treatment under U.S. tax law, so any gains or income the RRSP has earned by the time you cross the border is simply added to your cost, or "basis," in the plan.

In short, the basis is the value of the plan at the time you immigrate to the U.S. (ignoring any unrealized gains or losses at that time).[13] Income earned after immigration is deferred for U.S. tax purposes under the treaty, but it does not increase the basis.

The U.S. allows a recipient to deduct a portion of the "basis" in the plan upon each withdrawal. If you make a withdrawal of 10 percent of the value of the plan, the U.S. will allow you to deduct 10 percent of the basis.

Finally, even though the U.S. recognizes a smaller amount of income than Canada does, the entire Canadian tax paid is eligible for a foreign tax credit on the U.S. return (subject to certain limits).

The individual state you move to may tax income in the RRSP, either each year as it is earned (on a "current basis" — California again), or upon withdrawal. Some states allow foreign tax credits; others do not.

Maximizing the Benefit of Your Deferred Income Plan
Here are some tips on how to get the most for the least:

- Maximize your contribution before leaving Canada.

- Realize all "pregnant" gains prior to immigration. Sell the winners (but keep them in the RRSP). Don't sell any losers until after you've left Canada.

- While resident in the U.S., retain your RRSP as long as possible. When you reach age 69, turn it into a RRIF or annuity so you can continue to defer the tax, and minimize the withholding on what you do have to take out. Take the minimum distributions. Once the money's out you can't put it back in.

- If you decide to return to Canada, consider withdrawing the remainder of the money before coming back. You need to decide whether the deferral advantage (keeping the money out of the taxman's hands for more years) is outweighed by the difference between the 25 percent rate and what you'll have to pay on a withdrawal as a Canadian resident (up to 53 percent).

- Report the RRSP or RRIF to the IRS. There's an election that has to be filed annually to get the benefit of the deferral.

CROSS-BORDER COLLECTION
Beware of "take-the-money-and-run" approaches to tax planning. One of the most important parts of the recent protocol to the treaty is an agreement between the countries that they will (in limited circumstances) enforce each other's tax laws.

Once a tax liability has been "finally determined" by Canada, upon request by Revenue Canada the U.S. will treat the debt as though it was to the IRS. The only time the IRS must refuse a request is when the individual was a U.S. citizen at the time the liability was incurred.

SUMMARY

Remember, this chapter is a brief overview of only some parts of a vast U.S. tax system. Tax advice doesn't come in a one-size-fits-all. The law is complex and constantly changing. Consult your advisor before moving to the U.S. or making any significant financial arrangements.

APPENDIX

Estate Tax Marginal Tax Rates[14]

Taxable Estate ($)	Rate (%)
Under 10,000	18
20,000	20
40,000	22
60,000	24
80,000	26
100,000	28
150,000	30
250,000	32
500,000	34
750,000	37
1,000,000	39
1,250,000	41
1,500,000	43
2,000,000	45
2,500,000	49
3,000,000	53
Excess	55

Unified Credit Against Estate Tax

Year	Estate covered by Unified Credit (U.S.$)
2,000	675,000
2,001	675,000
2,002	700,000
2,003	700,000
2,004	850,000
2,005	950,000
2,006 and subsequent years	1,000,000

Marginal Income Tax Rates — 2000

Canada & Ontario (Married, Spouse Earns No Income)		United States (Married, Filing Joint)	
Under C$30,004	23.55%	Under US$43,850	15.00%
$56,668	34.63%	$105,950	28.00%
$60,009	36.55%	$161,450	31.00%
$65,252	42.40%	$288,350	36.00%
$77,841	46.42%	Excess	39.60%
Excess	47.87%		
CPP+EI	6.2%	Social Security	7.65%
Maximum Salary	CPP 3.8% – 37,400	Maximum Salary	6.2%–$76,200
	EI 2.4% – 39,000		1.45%-no limit

Note:

- The U.S. rate of regular tax on capital gains is limited to 20 percent. Canada taxes only ²/₃ of capital gains.
- State taxes range from nil (Florida, Alaska, Nevada, South Dakota, Texas, Washington, Wyoming) to 12 percent (Massachusetts, North Dakota).
- Some cities also have taxes (New York City — 3.8276 percent for residents).

Where to Get IRS Forms

Internal Revenue Service
EADC
Carolina Avenue
Richmond VA
U.S.A, 23222
Telephone 800-829-3676
Internet: www.irs.ustreas.gov/forms_pubs/index.html

Individual Taxpayer Identification Number:
Internal Revenue Service
PCS—ITIN DP426
PO Box 447
Bensalem PA
U.S.A, 19020
Telephone 215-516-4846

Main International Service Centre:
Internal Revenue Service
Philadelphia PA
U.S.A, 19255

Notes

1. There are hundreds of certifying acceptance agents around the world. The International Tax Services Group, located in Toronto, is one.
2. All figures in U.S. dollars except where noted.
3. For 2000.
4. Form T1135.
5. See Appendix. Remember, the decedent is a non-resident alien for U.S. tax purposes.
6. Top marginal rate assumed.
7. Including corporations that are principally involved in real estate.
8. For 2000. See Appendix.
9. Figures in this paragraph are in Canadian dollars.
10. Using Canada/BC tax rates for 1996, and ignoring CPP, EI, and other income and deductions.
11. Subject to certain limits.
12. For 2000.
13. There is some uncertainty whether this also applies to Canadian pension plans, or to locked-in RRSPs (which are created by a transfer of money from a pension plan). The basis may be limited to the employee's contributions, the employer's contributions, the income earned on each portion, or some combination of these.
14. Current as of February 2000.

Chapter 6
International Tax Planning
— Harley Mintz, FCA —

Let's do a quiz. Which of the following is true? The way you save tax by going offshore is:

a. depositing your cash in a numbered Swiss bank account and not reporting the interest;

b. incorporating an operating company in Cayman, under a fictitious name;

c. investing in Japanese mutual funds and not bringing the money back to Canada.

If you guessed "none of the above," you win!

If it were that easy, we'd all be offshore. Contrary to popular belief (or wishful thinking), it isn't. That's because Canada taxes its residents on their worldwide income, no matter where it is earned. Furthermore, if a company is incorporated outside of Canada but is managed from inside Canada, it is considered resident here and therefore usually taxable in Canada — so frankly, the above techniques are tax evasion.

Now that you know what going offshore isn't, let's consider some of the things it is:

- an incredible opportunity for huge tax savings and deferrals.

- setting up a vehicle (usually a trust or corporation in an offshore jurisdiction).

- a structure in which tremendous attention must be paid to detail.

- expensive to set up.

Given the cost, going offshore is only worthwhile if significant funds can be sheltered from Canadian tax. Sometimes, all that can be achieved is a lengthy deferral of tax, rather than an absolute savings. Nonetheless, our attitude is a twist on an old adage, "a dollar deferred (long enough) is a dollar saved."

Why should you consider going offshore? There are three main reasons: one is tax minimization; the second is creditor proofing; and the third is to hedge against currency restrictions. In this chapter, we'll review only the first two. The third will be well covered in other chapters.

The top personal tax rate in most provinces is approximately 50%. If tax can successfully be avoided, your aftertax yield is effectively doubled! And the savings are even greater if the tax rate increases further, which it inevitably does with alarming regularity. In addition to tax savings on the income, it may be possible to transfer the capital appreciation offshore so that it escapes Canadian capital gains tax. This may also reduce probate fees, as well as succession duties, should the provinces reintroduce estate taxes.

The best way to illustrate the possibilities and savings in going offshore is by example. With respect to moving investment income offshore, there are several scenarios in which even Revenue Canada would agree that the income is not taxable in Canada. There are several more in which Revenue Canada would certainly not be so agreeable.

Let's start with what I call the "strictly kosher" scenarios. These entail the use of non-resident trusts.

A trust consists of a settlor who creates it and the trustees who manage it on behalf of the beneficiaries. A trust is resident where the trustee who manages the trust resides, or if there is more than one trustee, where the majority of the trustees reside. A non-resident trust that earns passive-type income, such as interest, rents, and capital gains, is taxable in Canada only if two conditions are met. First, the beneficiaries are Canadian residents, and second, the money in the trust comes from a person who was resident in Canada. If you can stay out of either one of these conditions, opportunities abound! For example, if a father lives in Hong Kong and his daughter in Canada, the father can establish an offshore trust with his daughter as beneficiary. The father could gift money to the trust to be invested in mutual funds and there would be no Canadian tax on the gains. After a few years, the money can be distributed to the daughter from the trust as capital, so it comes into Canada tax free.

For those who do not have such generous relatives living offshore, some aggressive planners employ a variation of this theme. They have a Canadian gift funds to a friendly non-resident, who then establishes the trust for the Canadian's kids. I don't know about you, but this doesn't pass the smell test for me.

Another way to avoid Canadian taxation is for a Canadian resident to settle an offshore trust for a beneficiary who is not resident in Canada. For example, a mother residing in Toronto can set up an offshore trust for her son living in, say, England and transfer her cash to the trust. The trust invests in debt or equity investments, even certain Canadian investments. There will be no Canadian tax on the trust's income.

There are two further exceptions to the condition that the money must not come from a Canadian resident. One is that if the Canadian resident who puts the money into the trust has been in Canada for less than 60 months, the trust is not taxable here until the 60 months has been reached. Using the 60-month rule, immigrants to Canada can place their own assets in an offshore trust and move to Canada. For the first five years (i.e., 60 months), there is no tax in Canada on such income. If the Canadian resident requires money, the trust could distribute its capital tax free.

The second refinement is that if you were a Canadian resident and then leave Canada, once you're gone for 18 months, subsequent income earned in an offshore trust you set up is not taxable in Canada. So, using the 18-month rule, an emigrant from Canada can settle a non-resident trust for relatives who remain in Canada and, starting 18 months later, the income isn't taxable in Canada.

In dealing with immigrant trusts, we often use a structure whereby the trust owns a non-resident corporation in which the funds are placed to avoid certain adverse Canadian tax rules.

That is the "kosher" planning. Now for the "not-quite-so-kosher" planning! Let's say the money and the beneficiaries are in Canada, and there are no generous non-resident relatives. Can anything be done? There are very aggressive and complex plans that rely on tiny cracks in the Income Tax Act to avoid Canadian taxation. For example, a Canadian father could settle a non-resident trust which could have, say, the International Red Cross as its beneficiary. The income earned in the trust would not be taxed in Canada, so the argument goes, because there are no Canadian beneficiaries. Years later, when the family moves out of Canada, the beneficiaries would be changed to, perhaps, the children, and the funds extracted tax free. You should be warned that many (but not all) commentators believe this to be tax evasion if the father's intention was always to name his kids as the beneficiaries.

By the way, in this scenario you might wonder how you can be sure the trustees will change the beneficiary when asked, given that they control the trust. Here we introduce the concept of the protector — the person who can, by contract, hire and fire the trustees. The protector should be a non-resident and very, very trustworthy.

I know what you are wondering: OK, so I manage to earn all my money in a nontaxable offshore trust. What do I do with it all? You invest it, and when you're ready, there are ways for you to bring it home tax free so you can spend it.

Unlike investment income, active business income can be earned in an offshore company without attracting Canadian tax:

- If the funds earned by an active offshore business will be required back in Canada, it is usually advisable to incorporate in a country which has a very low, or no, tax rate and with which Canada has a tax treaty. This is to enable funds to be repatriated from the offshore company to its Canadian parent. This can be done on a tax-free basis only if the offshore company is in a treaty jurisdiction.

- The offshore company must actually perform the functions for which it is being paid. In order to "give life" to the offshore company so that it can handle the tasks, it must either have employees or retain a local agent to carry out these functions.

- The offshore company must not be managed from within Canada. In tax parlance, the "mind and management" of the offshore company must be offshore. Directors' meetings must be held, and decisions must be made, outside of Canada. This is often done by appointing three directors, one of whom would be a member of the Canadian resident's family and two of whom would be resident in the offshore jurisdiction.

Only certain types of business income can be earned offshore without being taxed in Canada. Generally, it is no longer possible to set up offshore buying companies to purchase goods internationally and resell them to a related Canadian company at a markup. However, it is still possible to set up a company offshore to export goods from Canada to other parts of the world.

Let's assume Jayco is a Canadian manufacturer with sales of $10 million which exports $5 million of finished goods to Europe and sells $5 million locally. A new company, Barbados Inc., would be incorporated in the Barbados as a subsidiary of Jayco. The finished goods will be purchased from Jayco by Barbados Inc., but shipped to Europe. Barbados Inc. would handle tasks such as marketing, financing, and the warranty of goods. With respect to these services, Barbados Inc. could earn a markup of, say, 10% on the value of the goods passing through it.

In the case of Jayco, this would transfer approximately $500,000 of profit offshore. Barbados has a very low local income tax rate — currently 2.5% for an international business corporation. The tax savings in using the structure is almost a quarter-million dollars annually! There are savings in using this structure even if the money is needed back in Canada. The aftertax monies could be returned to Canada as a dividend, free from Barbados withholding tax, and received by Jayco on a tax-free basis.

Unless and until the monies are required for the personal use of the Canadian individual shareholders of Jayco, all Canadian taxes can be deferred until Jayco is sold or until the death of the shareholders and their spouses. If the funds were needed for personal use, a dividend could be paid from Jayco to the shareholders. This dividend would be subject to the Canadian gross-up and tax-credit mechanism, resulting in a tax rate of approximately 35%. This is a 15% savings over the 50% tax rate applicable if the monies were earned in a country with which Canada does not have a tax treaty, or in *Canada itself.*

In the past, we used to say 50% of good offshore tax planning was never having to face questions from Revenue Canada. The other 50% was having good answers if you did. Unfortunately, the first 50% may no longer be available. In the February 1995 budget Finance Minister Martin announced that, for taxation years starting after 1999, if you have investments outside Canada, you will be required to disclose certain information about them. To summarize, these obligations are extensive and will require

- taxpayers with interests in foreign bank accounts, shares, real estate, etc., with a cost in excess of $100,000, to provide details of their holdings (splitting amongst related taxpayers seems to work);

- beneficiaries of most types of non-resident trusts to file an information return if they receive any distributions in the year; and

- people who transfer or lend property to a non-resident trust to file an information return. And some of the information is retroactive to 1991!

Significant exclusions for the $100,000 disclosure are:

- property used in an active business;

- personal use property; and

- property held in registered retirement savings plans, registered retirement income funds, and registered pension plans.

The form was done by April 30, 1999. In addition to the world asset disclosure, world income must also be included. This means that many offshore trusts must be disclosed and the income reported to Revenue Canada. Financial and tax advisors are now legally liable for half of the penalties for assisting individuals who try to avoid taxes using questionable methods.

In decrying tax evaders, the Revenue Minister said, "These new rules were introduced because it would be unfair if we allowed some in our society to hide financial assets offshore to avoid paying taxes."

Do you think these rules will be effective in curbing tax evasion? You're not reporting your income, but you'll fill in the information return to let Revenue Canada know? I don't think so.

In offshore tax planning, there are many variations and permutations that can be used. Some have no downside — even if the structure is challenged successfully by Revenue Canada, you end up in the same tax position as if the transaction wasn't done, except for the nondeductible interest on the reassessed taxes. Nothing ventured, nothing gained. Others do have a significant downside. Offshore tax planning is not for the faint of heart, but, if successful, the tax savings can be enormous. As Mark Twain said, the difference between a taxidermist and tax collector is that the taxidermist takes only your skin!

Choosing the appropriate location for going offshore is important. Obviously, a low tax in the foreign jurisdiction is critical. If a tax treaty with Canada is a requirement, Cyprus and Barbados will likely be your choices. Where a treaty is not vital to the success of the tax plan, Bahamas, Turks, Cayman, Liechtenstein, the Channel Islands, Isle of Man, and several other countries become possibilities.

While your physical presence in the chosen offshore jurisdiction may be limited, in selecting a jurisdiction it is nonetheless advisable to consider eight factors:

1. Weather

2. Communications

3. Language

4. Banking and other institutions

5. Time zones

6. Political stability

7. Receptiveness to foreign investment

8. Availability of experienced advisors

A corollary purpose in going offshore is to creditor-proof the assets once you have created them. Creditor proofing is protecting your assets from your creditors. Because of the liability of directors, the difficulty professionals and manufacturers have in obtaining adequate insurance coverage against malpractice and product liability, the significant decline in the value of real estate, and the number of failed marriages, creditor proofing is on the increase. If you can't restructure your finances, creditor proofing may be your only alternative.

Creditor proofing can be achieved by the creation of an asset-protection trust designed to protect the assets in the trust from creditors of the person who contributes property to the trust, or of the beneficiaries. Asset-protection trusts have been used for a variety of reasons, ranging from matrimonial to political. It is common for European interests to seek to protect their assets outside their countries of residence from policies introduced by changing governments.

Because of extremely favourable legislation in a number of offshore jurisdictions, Canadians may find it useful to use an offshore trust formed in a tax haven with liberal trust legislation, including specific asset protection provisions. The Cook Islands, the Bahamas, Belize, and the Cayman Islands are examples of jurisdictions with favourable tax regimes and which have enacted specific legislation for asset-protection trusts.

In order to be able to attack an asset-protection trust in, for example, the Bahamas, a creditor must prove that the transfer to the trust was made with an intent to defraud. The burden of proving an intent to defraud is on the creditor. Furthermore, no action can be commenced unless if it is commenced within two years of the date of the transfer to the trust. It may not be easy for a creditor even to find out about your assets in that time period. Bahamian laws provide that assets held by a Bahamian asset-protection trust will be governed by Bahamian laws and that a foreign law purporting to influence the transaction is irrelevant.

Given the intent provision as well as various Canadian laws, the only really effective time to establish an asset-protection trust is before a liability to a creditor exists. Such a trust is most effective if the trust property is located outside of Canada and at least one of the trustees is resident in the jurisdiction where the trust is formed. If the assets remain in Canada, a Canadian court could permit the execution of a judgement against the offshore trust, notwithstanding its jurisdiction.

Offshore planning is a minefield. If you're not careful, you'll get blown up. But there are significant rewards for those who can successfully traverse the field. Another quiz: which of the following is true? Going offshore can:

- save you taxes

- protect your assets

- lead to fun in the sun

If you guessed all of the above, you win!

Chapter 7

Offshore Planning:
Alternatives and Implications

— Christopher V. Radomski, B.Sc., J.D., LL.B. —

You may have heard of the infamous Swiss bank account and have been told stories involving large suitcases bulging with cash being flown to far-off places where secrecy is the order of the day and the word "taxes" is not in the vocabulary. More recently, Hollywood has glamorized the use of offshore tax havens as places where sophisticated modern-day criminals do their business, and in the end the advisors find themselves faced with moral and sometimes life-threatening dilemmas.

With these images in your mind, and no thanks to the prohibitive tax situation in North America, you become bombarded with ads bringing the promise of "No Tax" and "Build Your Wealth Tax Free." With obvious anticipation you begin to explore the unknown world of offshore tax havens. You ask the questions, "What do these strange and far-off places have to offer for the average Canadian looking to put away some of their wealth and build it free from the grasp of the government's hungry tax collectors?" and, "Can tax havens become part of my overall estate plan?" Yes, offshore tax havens can offer many legitimate advantages, and yes, these havens can aid your domestic estate and financial plan.

As with any novel and topical area of financial planning, there is no shortage of information available to the public. Suddenly, offshore planning experts are popping up all over your neighbourhood peddling schemes enabling you to rid yourself of the horrible burden of tax. You begin to think how easy and prosperous life can be now that you won't be required to pay tax on your investments. Of course, the only regret you will have is that you didn't take advantage of this sooner in your life. Why, you could have been retired by now.

If you have been nodding your head in agreement and rubbing your hands in contentment, you should proceed with caution. It is all too attractive and enticing to convince yourself, or be convinced, that what you are about to engage in is legal and that you will not have any obligations to the revenue authorities. All too often, individuals will not consider their domestic tax implications as they are romanticized by the idea of roaming the world and not being accountable to any taxing authority. Offshore planning should be undertaken only if the circumstances justify it. A good rule of thumb is that if the program sounds too simple and easy to implement there may be immediate or future liability. This is especially the case if your first and only line of defence is premised upon no one ever finding out about your offshore bank account or company.

Throughout this chapter we will be living vicariously through our friend John Haven. John will be experiencing many lifestyle and financial changes and will serve as an example to illustrate the advantages and possible pitfalls of offshore planning. Currently, John Haven is 52 years of age, he is residing in Oakville, Ontario, and is preparing for an early retirement.

He currently owns a home in Oakville worth approximately $500,000, a cottage near Orillia worth $200,000, has an RSP in excess of $200,000 and has various investments held with his financial planner in excess of $1,000,000.

John has many concerns; namely, he wishes to spend time travelling and perhaps residing outside of Canada. He is concerned that the wealth he has built up in his lifetime will be susceptible to the hungry taxing authorities. John not only wants to spend the balance of his life living well but also wishes to pass on as much wealth to his son and daughters as possible.

John Haven could be considered an offshore planner's dream. His asset base, style of life and joie de vivre make him a very good candidate to move some or all of his assets offshore. As you read on further in this chapter you will see what advantages John may legitimately avail himself of offshore.

Fortunately for Canadians, not all avenues of offshore planning have been closed off. Individuals continue to structure their affairs offshore both on a personal and a corporate level. For some, offshore planning can also be a very effective part of their estate plan. The development of the world financial and trade markets have mandated the use of offshore centres. Offshore financial centres can offer services and benefits which are not available domestically. Canadians have now been exposed to the benefits of legally structuring their affairs offshore and are taking full advantage of the benefits.

What Is "Offshore"?

The term "offshore" can have a number of definitions depending on what the requirements of the individual or corporation are. Take the example of our friend John Haven. John is a Canadian citizen and has lived in Canada for the past 20 years. He has recently inherited over a million dollars from his aunt who resided in Italy. John has made the decision that with the inheritance he is in the enviable financial position where future employment is at his own discretion. John now embarks on a fact-finding mission which takes him to tax havens in the South Pacific, the Caribbean and Europe. John decides that suntanning and sailing are not his forte and he is not quite rich enough to move to Switzerland or Monaco. In any event, learning a new language reminds him of work. What are his options?

John has decided to engage in the most effective type of tax planning known to Canadians. He has decided to become a non-resident of Canada. Non-residency will be examined later in this chapter, but for now let's assume that John will become a non-resident of Canada and pay no further tax in Canada. John has good advisors so he realizes that he must establish residency somewhere in the world, and he has taken the time to visit various countries which will not tax him on his worldwide earnings.

For John, offshore means finding a jurisdiction that will grant him the right to reside without taxing him on his local or worldwide income. He may reside in countries such as the Turks and Caicos Islands or England (yes, England can be a tax haven for residency in certain situations).

There are a number of jurisdictions worldwide that offer some sort of tax, business or residency advantages. Most people would be surprised, for example, to be informed that the U.K. offered tax advantages. Because of the various offshore havens and types of transactions, the term "offshore" can be used in connection with any non-Canadian transaction or planning carried out for business, tax or personal enjoyment purposes.

Of course, most individuals envision lying on a beach with a cool drink, their beach house behind them built from the proceeds of their tax-free offshore investment fund, without a worry in the world, when they think of the term "offshore."

What Is an Offshore Tax Haven?

As illustrated by the example of the United Kingdom above, you may have broadened your perspective of what an offshore tax haven is. There are dozens of countries around the world that qualify as offshore tax havens in one form or another, and typically certain havens are best suited for specific financial transactions.

More specifically, a tax haven is a jurisdiction which imposes very little or no taxation whatsoever on its residents, whether individuals or corporations. To expand on this definition, there are certain havens that have geographic areas designated for tax-free transactions.

Tax havens may be divided into three categories:

1. "Complete" tax havens. These are tax havens in the truest sense, which impose zero personal or corporate tax. Examples of complete tax havens would include the Turks and Caicos Islands, the Bahamas, and the Cayman Islands;

2. Tax havens that impose a low level of tax. In these jurisdictions, individuals or corporations residing in the jurisdiction will pay a low amount of tax typically only on income generated in that jurisdiction. Examples of low tax havens would include the British Virgin Islands, the Channel Islands and Barbados;

3. A final category of tax haven would be the tax haven where specific financial transactions are encouraged. Examples of these havens would include Panama, the Netherlands Antilles and the U.K.

There is no universally accepted list of tax haven jurisdictions or financial centres, as tax experts and planners may have their preferred list of countries. As indicated above, depending on how you classify tax haven jurisdictions there can be as few as a dozen or as many as 65 tax haven jurisdictions worldwide.

The choice of jurisdiction to deal in can depend on many factors. It should be noted that many of the true non-tax haven jurisdictions have similar legislation and facilities. Here is a list of commonly referred-to tax haven jurisdictions:

Turks and Caicos Islands	British Virgin Islands
Liberia	Palau
Andorra	Campione

Liechtenstein

Netherlands Antilles

Luxembourg

Anguilla

Malaysia

Antigua and Barbuda

Malta

Aruba

Mauritius

Austria

Monaco

Bahamas

Montserrat

Nauru

Barbados

Western Samoa

Bermuda

Panama

Channel Islands

Nevis

Cook Islands

St. Vincent

Costa Rica

Seychelles

Cyprus

Sri Lanka

Gibraltar

Switzerland

Grenada

Hong Kong

United Kingdom

Ireland

Isle of Man

Cayman Islands

Factors for Consideration When Choosing a Tax Haven

As indicated above there can be a great many tax havens to consider worldwide. Below is a list of the factors that should be considered when choosing an offshore jurisdiction:

- quality of professional advisors

- favourable legislation

- political and economic stability

- exchange controls and currency

- tax treaties (if any)

- government attitude and investment incentives

- incorporation procedures

- telecommunication facilities

- legal base — common law or civil code

- secrecy and confidentiality

- banking facilities

- available professional services

- location and time zone

- type of business or transaction

The determination of which tax haven is best suited for any one person usually involves consideration of the above factors. One of the most important considerations is the reputation and track record of the offshore provider you decide to use. All too often clients will transfer funds offshore with either not having met their offshore provider or not having visited the jurisdiction in question to see the operation firsthand. Your offshore structure is only as solid as your offshore representative, and accordingly it makes very good sense to do some of the ground work yourself. As with any other type of financial transaction you should take great care in choosing your representatives.

Another important feature to consider when choosing your offshore provider is your representative's ability to comprehend and work within the laws of Canada. You will find offshore that the representatives come from varied backgrounds and a number of different countries. It is difficult to imagine how a U.K.-trained solicitor is properly qualified to give advice regarding U.S. tax matters or see how a Canadian lawyer is properly trained to give advice on U.K. tax issues. If you spend a little time and meet with the professionals offshore, you will find lawyers and accountants who have expertise in your market and can give you proper advice on your domestic issues. It is also highly recommended to seek the involvement of an independent domestic professional. Typically, an offshore firm can refer you to a local lawyer or accountant.

The costs involved in going offshore will depend on a number of factors. Obviously cost should be a consideration when choosing your offshore representative, but cost should not be the sole determination. Typically, due to the high overhead costs and the costs of doing business offshore generally, you will find that the larger organizations have higher fees as compared to smaller organizations. For example, most law firms offshore do not carry professional indemnity insurance.

My general impression is that you typically get what you pay for and usually there is a good reason why an organization has been in business for 20 years. Since offshore planning has become very topical in the past few years many small providers have popped up on the scene and are attempting to copy the services offered by the larger, more reputable organizations. There are definitely some small providers who offer very good services, but you should take care in their selection.

Confidentiality laws, or the lack thereof, in the jurisdiction you choose to do business in is also an important factor. Most of the offshore tax havens will have similar confidentiality laws but it must be stressed that confidentiality and secrecy are not a defence to a tax action. The confidentiality laws are designed to preserve the integrity and confidentiality of your personal financial matters — they were not designed as a shield to be used by unscrupulous individuals and international criminals.

It is important to note that many offshore jurisdictions are now enacting laws which will enable the domestic authorities to break through the confidentiality laws in situations where the client has committed a crime and the money offshore is a direct result of, or proceeds of, that crime. For the offshore jurisdiction to permit this to happen the crime has to be one which is punishable in the offshore jurisdiction. Conveniently, tax evasion is not an offence in offshore haven jurisdictions, as typically there is no form of personal or corporate taxation offshore. Therefore, if the money nestled in an offshore account should have been paid to a domestic taxing authority, the domestic authority will not have a claim or an ability to breach the confidentiality laws in the offshore jurisdictions under the current money-laundering legislation.

Why Structure Offshore

Estate and Tax Planning

Tax, tax, tax. Chances are that if you are conducting a word-association test most people would respond, "tax," in association with the terms "tax haven" "offshore," "Bahamas," "Cayman Islands," or any offshore jurisdiction. Yes, tax is still the main motivation for individuals looking into offshore financial centres.

Many factors will determine whether or not a tax haven can be used legally in tax-mitigation schemes. All too often, tax havens are simply used to hide income from the revenue authorities, as the confidentiality and secrecy laws in most offshore tax havens foster this type of activity. However, as domestic taxing authorities implement new rules and regulations, the tax evader is finding himself in a very precarious and risky position.

Aside from the phenomena of hiding your money and running from the taxing authorities, there are still legal methods to implement tax havens for the purpose of tax reduction. This in itself is a very complicated area and will be addressed later in this chapter. However, it is fair to state that if an individual's circumstances and financial position are suitable, a tax haven can still be used in a very effective fashion by Canadians.

The proper offshore planning can definitely become part of your domestic estate plan. Many individuals have moved assets into foreign jurisdictions so that the assets do not form part of the domestic estate. Further, assets may be placed offshore into foreign trusts or corporations enabling a foreign trust, for example, to determine the ultimate recipient or beneficiary of the asset.

Asset Protection

In this age of increased creditor rights and frivolous litigation, tax havens are being utilized for the purpose of asset protection. Asset protection can be defined as the structuring of one's affairs in such a manner as to inhibit or prevent the attachment of their assets from a creditor challenge. A number of domestic asset-protection techniques exist that should be utilized by Canadians, such as corporations, transfers to spouses and family members and the leveraging of property. All of these serve to either reduce an individual's equity in an asset or completely separate the ownership of an asset from the individual.

If you consider yourself to be in a high liability position or profession you are best advised to at least implement some sort of domestic asset protection plan. When you consider the amount of frivolous litigation and large court judgements being awarded in the United States it has become apparent that domestic planning techniques are not sufficient to prevent the attachment of your assets by creditors. This has been the main motivation for the development of offshore asset-protection techniques. North Americans are now shifting ownership of their assets not only to domestic asset-protection structures but to offshore entities as well. In most cases, where ownership of an asset can be traced to a foreign asset-protection structure it will be the laws of the foreign jurisdiction which will determine whether or not the creditor will succeed in seizing the asset. As you would suspect, the laws of many offshore jurisdictions have been specifically created to discourage and prevent one from becoming a successful creditor.

Unfortunately for Canadians, many societal tendencies creep across the border from the United States and many believe that the days of frivolous litigation, ambulance chasing and unrealistic court judgements are upon us. Add paranoia into the mix and you may be a candidate for an offshore asset-protection structure.

Flexibility of Law

There are many cases where tax havens are utilized by international business people because the laws in the havens are far more flexible than domestic law. A good example would be the corporate laws in most offshore jurisdictions, where many of the requirements and duties normally found in domestic law are absent. This can be a great benefit to the international trading company or to the multinational corporation looking to form a subsidiary for financing purposes.

Estate Planning

Although Canada eliminated estate taxes in 1972 and essentially replaced them with capital gains tax, probate fees do exist in Canada, and your estate assets will be subject to a deemed disposition a the time of your death. With the fear of increased taxation in Canada, the potential rebirth of the estate tax can never be ruled out. Assets structured properly offshore will not form part of your estate in Canada and, accordingly, individuals are moving assets offshore for this purpose. Specific planning techniques will be outlined later in this chapter.

Diversification

Most planners would recommend diversification of investing to hedge against a fluctuating economy and political instability. If you believe this philosophy, and are the type of person who likes to spread their assets, it makes sense to have assets in several different jurisdictions. By doing this you minimize the risk of having all your assets subject to the whims of any one government body.

Many firmly believe that even if your offshore involvement begins and ends with a simple personal bank account, which you disclose, your assets in that account will at least be under your control and will be much more difficult to seize or confiscate, compared to having the assets in a domestic bank account.

Offshore Structures

As you continue with your education process and become familiar with the various tax havens available around the world, and the benefits and pitfalls of dealing in each particular jurisdiction, you are then faced with the question, "What do I do in these havens anyway?"

This is a very interesting area because while there are typically three main vehicles that are utilized offshore, you will find that there are dozens of combinations and permutations of these three vehicles. These vehicles are the offshore bank account, the offshore company and, more recently, the offshore trust. Depending on the opinion and knowledge level of your advisor, you will be presented with structures that involve these three entities, some of which are very straightforward and basic, and some of which will be very complicated derivatives. The key is to understand the benefits and pitfalls of each entity and its particular application to you.

Offshore Bank Account

As indicated earlier, the offshore bank account is the classic form of offshore structure. Individuals would simply fill their Samsonites full of cash, take a flight to a faraway place and meet with a very gracious banker who would be delighted to take their suitcases off their hands and make investments for them. Due to the high degree of secrecy and confidentiality in these jurisdictions, these investors would be assured that no one would ever know they had opened an account, and of course no one would know of any income generated there. In many cases, even family members were unaware of these "secret" accounts, and one wonders who received the benefit of the cash when the account holder died.

The formation of an offshore bank account is relatively straightforward and many banks around the world are happy to do business with you. As time has passed, however, it has become very rare to find a bank willing to accept the proverbial Samsonite full of cash, as the more legitimate jurisdictions and banks will not allow this type of practice to be carried on anymore. As with many other areas of offshore finance, the international authorities are putting pressure on the offshore banks not to accept cash in an attempt to weed out the drug traffickers and money launderers.

So now you have selected a proper jurisdiction, you have flown there and met with the various banks and you have decided to open an offshore bank account. Typically, the bank will ask for at least one professional and/or bank reference from you. Further, the bank will usually ask for a notarized copy of your passport. The banks are concerned that you are a real person and that you have an established banking relationship somewhere in the world.

There are situations where a prospective client is reluctant to produce a bank letter of reference, as it typically has to be addressed to the offshore bank. The client is concerned that word will go out in their local branch that they requested a reference, and their whole town will know about their offshore bank account. This is usually magnified by the fact that the offshore bank account will probably be used for tax-evasion purposes; the client is unwilling to request such a letter feeling that by doing so they will be admitting to the domestic bank that they are intending to engage in some sort of illegal activity. There are many reasons to request a bank letter of reference and most clients are able to produce a reference. However, tax evaders should be paranoid.

The requirements above are necessary if an individual is going to be a signatory on any offshore bank account. If you decide to open a bank account within a corporation and you will be the signatory on the corporate account, you will be facing the same bank requirements.

The reluctance shown by individuals with respect to producing these documents is understandable. However, you will find that these requirements serve as a weeding-out process by banks and by offshore advisors. If a client is reluctant to produce letters of reference or documents attesting to their good character then most professionals consider them to be high-risk clients and not worth dealing with. Banks have a very similar view. In fact, you will find that some banks will request a minimum of two bank references and one professional reference, as well as other identifying documents to be produced for the formation of a personal or corporate bank account.

Offshore Companies
Offshore companies may be referred to as exempt companies, IBCs or offshore holding companies, to name a few. Regardless of what label is attached to them, they are all essentially the same thing. An offshore company is a company which is formed typically in a no-tax jurisdiction where it is very difficult to ascertain who is the true owner of the company.

Offshore companies are typically used for investment. In this case, a client will form the company, transfer assets offshore to the corporate bank account, and trade securities. It is important to note that if the client controls the company, holds any class of shares or has a nominee hold the shares for them, they will be faced with a taxable liability if the company generates income.

Exempted companies are of significant importance in jurisdictions such as the Turks and Caicos Islands, Bahamas and the Cayman Islands. In each of these jurisdictions an exempted company is not subject to any local taxes and enjoys special privileges. An exempt company is

- a separate legal person or legal entity;
- an entity which may continue indefinitely;
- an entity which can be controlled by one or more individuals;
- an entity which limits liability.

Attributes of exempt companies are as follows:

- may have nominee directors and shareholders
- need not disclose the amount of capital nor the beneficial shareholders of the company
- annual general meetings are not required

- must have at least one director and one secretary
- may move its domicile to another jurisdiction
- undertaking may be granted by the government conferring 20 years tax-free status
- bearer shares are permitted
- special confidentiality provisions apply
- the objects of the company can be unlimited

You may have noticed the term "nominee" mentioned above. It is important to understand the concept of a nominee. A nominee is an individual or corporation standing in the place of the client or directing mind of the company. The nominee director, for example, typically will take instructions directly from the client.

The majority of offshore companies are incorporated having nominees as directors, officers and original shareholders of record. The use of a nominee in these capacities enables the offshore professional to carry out transactions on behalf of the company and the nominee concept shields the true ownership and directing mind of the offshore company from inquiring minds. Be aware that the use of a nominee shareholder is not a tax structure.

Figure 1 sets out the basic structure of the offshore exempt company. You will note that options have been listed in reference to the share ownership of the company.

Figure 1: Anatomy of an Offshore Company

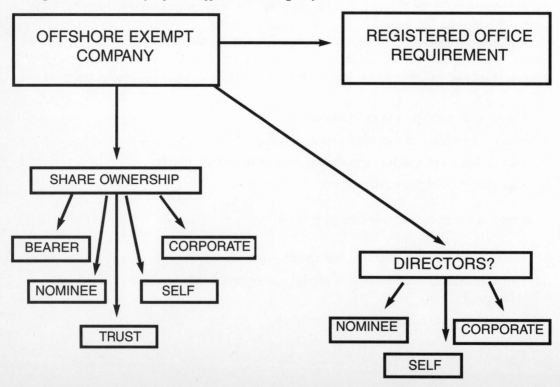

Offshore Trusts

As offshore planning becomes more sophisticated and planners are becoming more cognizant of the revenue rules in Canada, the use and application of offshore trusts has become commonplace. It is widely accepted among planners that the formation of an offshore company by a resident Canadian will definitely have adverse tax implications. Accordingly, planners have been looking at new techniques and vehicles in an effort to work within the tax rules put forth by Revenue Canada.

The word "trust" can mean a number of different things. For example, a solicitor may hold shares of a company in trust for the client. This trust is evidenced by a simple one- or two-page agreement and states that "I, John Attorney, hold the shares of ABC Limited for the benefit of John Haven." This can be contrasted with a true trust which creates a legal relationship between a trustee, a beneficiary and the individual who creates the trust, the settlor.

To properly understand the concept of a trust, one must first understand the idea of separation of interests with respect to assets. To illustrate, if you personally are on title for a piece of real estate in Ontario, you will be the legal registered owner as well as the beneficial owner of the property. Considering the example above with the solicitor holding shares of a company in trust for a client, the attorney may be the registered or legal shareholder of the company, but they are holding the shares for the benefit of the client. In this instance, the attorney would be the legal titleholder, but the client would be the beneficial holder to the shares.

The important concept to keep in mind when thinking of trusts is that an individual or an entity may be the registered holder of the assets but they may be simply holding the asset for the benefit of a third party. Clearly, there are two interests in the property — the legal interest as well as the beneficial interest. The holder of the legal and beneficial interests may have taxable implications and, accordingly, it is very important to consider the residency of these individuals.

When creating a trust, the individual who places assets into the trust, the "settlor," typically relinquishes the legal and beneficial title to these assets. The legal title to the assets will typically rest with the trustee and the trust document itself will determine who has beneficial title, these being the beneficiaries.

An individual forming a trust is in a sense giving up all ownership rights to the assets, whether future or immediate, and placing confidence in the trustee to preserve and manage these assets for a named group of beneficiaries. You may find that there is an additional position or individual named in an offshore trust, the "protector," whose task is to typically guard against misappropriations by the trustee.

An offshore trust should not be confused with a share trust agreement or share warrant agreement. A share trust agreement is an agreement where an individual or company holds shares in trust for another individual. A share warrant agreement is an agreement where an individual has an immediate or future right to purchase the shares of a company which are registered to a nominee shareholder.

The parties commonly found in an offshore trust are the following:

1. Settlor

The settlor is the individual or individuals who transfer or give property to the trust. You will find in some offshore trust arrangements that an unrelated party who has not contributed assets to the trust is named as a settlor for tax-planning purposes. In this instance, the revenue authorities would most likely deem the true contributor of the funds as the settlor.

2. Offshore Trustee

The trustee holds legal title to the property found within the trust. You will find that there are many groups offshore holding themselves out as trustees, so you should ensure that the trustee you select is a bona fide trustee, licensed, regulated and insured in the jurisdiction in which they reside. Insurance and regulation are important features, as the trustee is accountable for the preservation of the assets and must act in the best interest of the trust. They are accountable for negligent acts and clearly have a fiduciary duty to the trust. Be aware of the single-purpose trust company.

3. Beneficiaries

The beneficiaries are those groups or individuals who will ultimately benefit from the property. The trust document itself will determine when and how the assets will pass to the beneficiaries and typically, the offshore trust document will provide for the ability to change or substitute beneficiaries as time goes on.

4. Protector

The protector is an individual named in the trust deed who is typically granted a group of specific powers. These powers may include the ability to change the trustee, the ability to change the jurisdiction of the trust, and a veto power of distributions made by the trustee.

The key to an offshore trust from a taxation perspective is its ability to separate the legal and beneficial interests to the assets. This a feature not found with companies and enables the planner to work within the tax rules under certain circumstances. It is common in offshore trust structures to find that an offshore company has been incorporated and the shares of that offshore company have been conveyed to that offshore trust. This is set out in Figure 2.

Trusts may be utilized for estate planning and tax planning, as well as asset protection. From an estate planning perspective, assets conveyed to the trust may not form part of the individual's estate in their home country. The distribution of those assets will be determined by the trust itself and distribution does not have to occur at the death of the settlor.

The principal objective for creating a trust for asset-protection purposes is to insulate your assets from the threat of a future creditor or court judgement. Laws have been formed in various offshore jurisdictions that specifically inhibit the ability of creditors to seize assets based on a foreign judgement. The laws in these offshore jurisdictions specifically set out the rules and tests the creditor must satisfy in the foreign courts before they are able to obtain any assets at the end of the day. Typically, retaining counsel in a faraway

Figure 2: Offshore Trust Structure

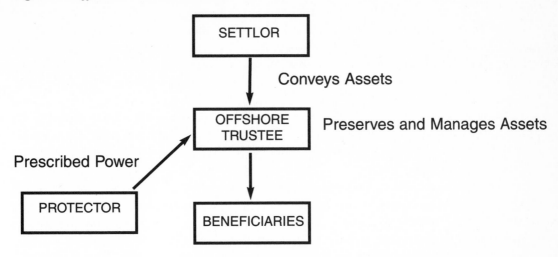

country in an attempt to circumvent stringent anti-creditor laws is neither cost effective nor fruitful to the creditor. For these reasons challenges typically never occur.

From a tax perspective, trusts are commonly used in conjunction with an offshore holding company. Please refer to Figure 3. In this instance, the shares of the offshore holding company will be conveyed to the trust and accordingly the trustee will hold title to the company. It is common for assets to be held within the company for the purposes of investment.

Figure 3: Sample Offshore Structure

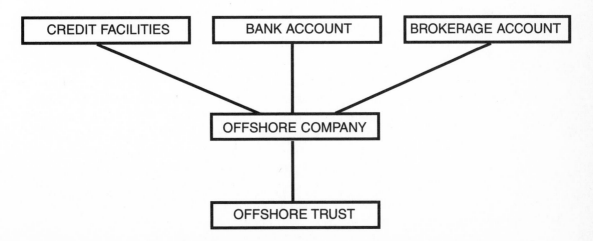

Canadian Tax Considerations

The use and misuse of offshore structures has become prominent in both the United States and Canada in recent years. I say "misuse," as many offshore arrangements have been created under the guise of a trust or arms-length corporation, but in fact are no more than sham relationships contrived to fool domestic authorities. The key to effective offshore planning is to receive the best possible advice and representation both onshore and offshore, and to ensure that all relevant local laws are abided by.

Too often, situations arise where potential clients state they are onside with the tax authorities since no information will ever be disclosed. It should be stressed that confidentiality and secrecy have never been defences to a tax action and should not be relied upon heavily by the client.

In certain circumstances, planning techniques do exist that will permit the legitimate and effective use of offshore trusts by North Americans. Again, potential clients should be aware that they must investigate and consider the application of their domestic laws in relation to any offshore planning they are considering. Further, the client should ensure that they have complied with their domestic legislation.

Significant legislation is currently in existence affecting the formation and taxation of foreign entities. In addition, recent amendments have been made to the Income Tax Act (ITA) which may have direct application to offshore structures.

The main provisions or sections of the ITA that apply to offshore structures would include the "FAPI" rules, sections 75, 94, and 248 of the ITA, as well as the new foreign reporting rules. Of course, s.245, GAAR, may always have potential application to tax-planning structures. The rules are far too exhaustive for a detailed examination here, but the main ideas will be covered.

When considering the tax implications of an offshore structure, you should keep in mind the differences between *legal* and *beneficial* ownership of a company, trust or asset offshore. Typically, if you are the beneficial owner of a foreign asset of company, or beneficially interested in a trust, you will most likely have some sort of reporting requirement to Revenue Canada, or in fact have income attributable to you for taxation purposes.

Trusts

A trust is deemed to be resident in the jurisdiction where the majority of the trustees who control the trust reside. Accordingly, one must consider the jurisdiction of the trustee. Further, if your trust has a "protector," the residence and powers of the protector will be important in the determination of the residence of the trust.

The powers conferred on the protector may be reactive powers or proactive powers. The protector may be considered to control the trust, with the result that the trust may be found to be resident in the jurisdiction where the protector resides. Obviously, if the protector resides in Canada, the trust may be deemed a Canadian trust for tax purposes. If the trust is deemed to be Canadian, then the trust would be taxable in Canada.

Under subsection 94(1) of the Income Tax Act, certain non-resident trusts may be deemed to be resident in Canada where the following conditions are met:

a. a person beneficially interested in the trust is resident in Canada; and

b. the trust acquired property directly or indirectly in any manner whatsoever from the beneficiary referred to in (a), or someone related to that beneficiary, provided that such beneficiary or related person was resident in Canada in the 18-month period preceding the transfer of property to the trust and that person had been resident in Canada for a total of 60 months.

The term "beneficially interested" is defined very broadly in the ITA and can mean any immediate or future right.

These sections of the ITA can have very broad application and typically trap many so-called offshore trusts. Many individuals are finding themselves in situations where they thought or were advised that their foreign trusts would never be taxable in Canada, while all along their trusts could be deemed Canadian for income tax purposes. Obviously this would be counterproductive to the whole exercise of creating a foreign trust.

Revenue Canada — New Reporting Rules

The Department of Finance has released legislation requiring Canadian residents to report transfers, which would include gifts, to offshore trusts. These foreign reporting requirements received Royal Assent on April 25, 1997, as Bill C-92. The new provisions require taxpayers to report

- interests in foreign property in excess of C$100,000 (this was suspended until the 1999 tax year);
- interests in foreign affiliates;
- transfers or loans to non-resident trusts; and
- distributions from non-resident trusts.

The new reporting rules brought forth by Revenue Canada serve to restrict various areas of offshore planning, primarily by requiring disclosure of certain events. Essentially, you may be required to report to Revenue Canada when funds are transferred to an offshore jurisdiction, and you must also report certain interests you may have in offshore entities, those being interests in trust and companies. The new reporting rules also require Canadian beneficiaries who receive a distribution from a foreign trust to report the distribution.

It should be kept in mind that the new reporting rules simply require disclosure of certain events. It may be that the event that is disclosed will not result in tax being attributed to a Canadian, but Revenue Canada nevertheless wants to know that the event has occurred. Obviously, if someone has transferred funds or set up an offshore structure and they are counting on secrecy to be their shield from the Revenue Canada authorities, they will most likely be caught under one of the new reporting requirements. The best planning techniques will legally alleviate any requirement for disclosure and any potential attribution of tax back to Canada.

The taxation of foreign corporations and trusts is a very complicated area and you should consult an expert in the field prior to engaging in any type of offshore activity. As a starting point, you should consider whether or not you are the beneficial owner of an offshore company or are beneficially interested in a foreign trust created by a Canadian. If you fall into either of these two categories, there may be a taxable implication for you in Canada. Again, it should be stressed that the mere fact the authorities will not find out about your offshore company is neither an excuse nor a justification not to report your interests to Revenue Canada. Viable planning opportunities do exist for those who take the time and effort to structure their affairs properly.

Asset Protection

Asset-protection planning can be defined simply as the organizing of one's assets and affairs in advance as a precautionary measure to protect against future risks. Like other forms of trust planning, asset-protection planning is not a new phenomenon. Various forms of family and corporate planning have long been used to achieve similar goals.

The onslaught of frivolous litigation in the United States, unfortunately to be followed in Canada, has created a new awareness of the threat wealthy individuals face. Planners are now considering methods to shield their clients' assets in the event they are met in the future with an unforeseen creditor threat.

From an American perspective, asset-protection planning is carried out on a tax-neutral basis; that is, information is disclosed to the taxing authorities and relevant taxes are paid on a yearly basis. The clear motivation is not to mitigate taxes, but to isolate one's assets from future challenges.

Sophisticated asset-protection planning for Canadians is becoming increasingly popular as more Canadians realize that society is becoming more litigious and that their assets may be at risk.

There are various tools that may be utilized in asset-protection structures, both domestic and foreign. Domestic vehicles would include joint ownership, insurance, limited life companies, domestic trusts and family limited partnerships. Probably the most effective method of asset-protection planning is expatriation, but this is not always the most convenient.

Foreign-domiciled asset-protection trusts, when used in conjunction in domestic tools, have grown to become very effective vehicles to insulate individuals' assets from future creditor challenges. Planners will not only draft the appropriate trust, but will look to offshore jurisdictions with laws specifically designed to foster the protection of one's assets through an asset-protection trust. The Turks and Caicos is one such jurisdiction. The Turks and Caicos Islands has finalized the drafting of legislation which provides concrete protection for trusts settled within the islands.

As with any other type of planning, the client should receive advice and comply with respect to domestic fraudulent preference laws. Essentially, a client must keep in mind that an asset-protection structure is a preventative measure and not a cure to a pending action.

Emigration of Canadian Resident Individuals

Tax Issues
In response to the fleeing of assets from Canada, Revenue Canada has made it difficult and possibly costly to become a non-resident of Canada. A departure tax has been created, and accordingly it is important that, prior to becoming a non-resident of Canada, each of your assets be examined to determine whether or not immediate tax is payable or some sort of guarantee must be provided to ensure that the tax will be paid. This may be the case whether or not you dispose of your assets before leaving Canada.

Essentially, almost all of your property will be subject to this departure tax except Canadian real property (that is, real estate), and capital property used in a Canadian business. The balance of your property may be subject to a deemed disposition at a fair market value immediately before you leave Canada. You must either pay the tax or post security with Revenue Canada if you are unable to pay the tax immediately. (See also "Strategies for Emigration from Canada" in chapter 5, page 94.)

Practical Issues of Immigration
There are many issues and factors you should think about, outside of the tax considerations, when deciding to become a non-resident. Sure, it is very attractive to picture yourself sitting on the beach in a tax haven jurisdiction, but having lived in such a jurisdiction for a number of years, I will tell you that the lifestyle may not be for everyone.

There is no doubt that the tax advantages of living in a tax haven jurisdiction can be incredible. However, governments in the tax havens do levy duties on almost all goods you import and require you to pay fees every year for the right to reside in their country. As well, you will not find developed health care programs in these countries and will be required to provide for your independent medical coverage. If you are in fairly good health, this is not too costly; however, this is something you must factor into your decision.

Depending on the country which you choose to live in, you will have to do without some or most of the conveniences you have become accustomed to in North America. For example, some of the tax havens do not have any movie theatres; some have limited medical services; and the quality of food may be less than what you are used to in Canada. However, knowing that you will never be faced with having to get up early to clean the snow off your car, you may be willing to make certain sacrifices.

There has clearly been an increase in residency applications in the Turks and Caicos Islands. There are many advantages to retiring to such a place, including an enormous tax benefit. Many offshore jurisdictions actively encourage ex-patriates to reside in their country, and in fact you will find a large Canadian contingent residing in the Turks and Caicos.

In selecting a foreign jurisdiction in which to reside, you will want to choose one that will not tax you on your local income and will definitely not tax you on your worldwide income. You may consider the Turks and Caicos Islands, Cayman Islands, Mexico, England, Ireland or Costa Rica. Each of these jurisdictions will have certain advantages and disadvantages and should be examined in light of your individual needs.

Case Studies

John Haven will again be used as an example in the each of the three case studies to follow. John Haven can be described as

- 52 years of age;

- a resident of Ontario;

- an owner of a residence worth $500,000 and a cottage worth $200,000;

- having a son who resides in England;

- having two daughters who reside in British Columbia;

- currently separated from his wife who resides with the two daughters;

- having cash and securities in excess of $1,000,000;

- being in good health.

Case 1: Non-residency

John has decided to sever his Canadian residency. Since John will be departing Canada, he must file an income tax return and must pay Canadian tax on all income earned up to the time of his departure. He may have to pay certain departure taxes depending on the nature of his assets, but assuming that his home and cottage are tax-paid items, they will be free of tax. Tax is payable on the deemed disposition of his investments.

John must ensure that he has severed his Canadian residence, and in making this determination he must consider the following factors:

- presence of a residence in Canada

- family member and/or spouse living in Canada

- bank accounts and credit facilities in Canada

- golf and yacht club memberships

- presence of any Canadian mailing addresses

- presence of a Canadian driver's licence

- presence of a burial plot in Canada

Any one of these facts alone may not solely determine whether or not John is a resident for Canadian tax purposes; however, Revenue Canada will consider all of these factors when making a determination. Since John is not divorced from his wife, Revenue Canada may argue that he has significant family ties to Canada, thereby making him a Canadian resident. Obviously, John would argue that a divorce is imminent, and in any event he does not reside with his spouse or two daughters.

One of the most important factors in the determination of residency is the number of days John will spend in Canada. John must ensure that he will spend fewer than 182 days in any one given year in Canada. It is also recommended that he minimize his time in Canada during his first year as a non-resident. Further, if John decides to spend time in the United States, he should ensure that he spends no more than 122 days in any one given calendar year in the United States.

So now John has made the final decision and is structuring his living arrangements. John will sell his home and transfer his cottage into the names of his two daughters. From the proceeds of the sale of John's home, he has decided to rent a condominium in South Florida for three months of the year. John has also decided he will be purchasing a beach-front condominium in the Turks and Caicos Islands.

John has visited the Turks and Caicos Islands and decided that this jurisdiction is very suitable to him. Accordingly, he has filed for and received a two-year residency permit in the Islands. John is unsure about how much time he will spend in the Turks and Caicos, as he plans to do some travelling throughout Europe. He assumes that he will spend at least five months in the Islands.

Once John has established residency in the Islands, he proceeds to set up an exempt company and will open up bank and investment accounts so that he may reinvest all of the remaining funds he has moved out of Canada.

Case 2: Formation of an Offshore Trust

John has decided that he is not yet ready to move offshore, but he wishes to explore the formation of an offshore trust. He believes that his son living in the U.K. may afford him some planning opportunities, and he is correct.

John proceeds with the formation of an offshore trust and holding company. John will be the settlor of the trust, the trustee will reside in the Turks and Caicos and his son will be the beneficiary. John will retain very little if any right to determine the outcome of the assets once the trust has been created. Also, the trust will preclude the addition of any resident Canadian beneficiaries. John will consider non-residency in the future.

Case 3: Asset Protection

John has been involved in the mining business for the past few years and currently finds himself in the position of director of a publicly traded resource and mining company called BigDough. BigDough has become very successful and its stock price has been rising consistently over the past two years. Since John is a director of the company, he was able to purchase large blocks of stock in BigDough which he has recently sold for huge profits.

Unfortunately for John and BigDough, it has become apparent that the laboratory that tested the core samples from the properties owned by BigDough made an honest mistake and the sample contained copper, not gold. This creates an enormous amount of litigation, and of course the stock price of BigDough plummets. John, being a director, is named in the lawsuits, and it is being alleged that he intentionally misled the public with respect to BigDough.

If John's assets are all held in the same jurisdiction where the court actions are brought, and John is found to be liable either rightfully or wrongfully, his assets will be seized easily by the creditors. If, however, John had structured his assets in such a manner to take advantage of the offshore asset-protection laws, his creditors would have to firmly establish that he was involved in wrongdoing and intended to defraud them specifically before they could seize the assets.

If John had structured his affairs such that the majority of his domestic assets were owned by an offshore asset-protection trust (APT) and all assets were conveyed to this trust at a time when John was solvent and not in anticipation of litigation, he may have been able to insulate his wealth. The laws in some offshore jurisdictions provide for a statute of limitation on creditor challenges, i.e., if you convey your assets to an APT, and two years elapse without a challenge, the creditors may be statute barred from challenging the transfer of those assets offshore.

CONCLUSION

You may have formed the opinion that offshore planning is not as simple and straightforward as portrayed by some. The difficulty arises in drafting and planning in accordance and compliance with the relevant revenue rules in the client's home jurisdiction.

Viable estate and tax planning opportunities do exist for those whose position and future goals are suited to offshore planning. As indicated earlier, clients must receive competent planning advice and ensure that they comply with their domestic legislation. Due diligence should be carried out when investigating offshore structures and offshore service providers.

Chapter 8
Offshore Investing and Structuring

— Gordon Polovin —

The subject of international and offshore structuring and investment covers a vast, complex and diversified arena of financial activity. To simplify things, I will establish some goals and parameters at the outset to define a particular segment of the market

Goals

- To secure confidentiality and privacy in management of financial affairs
- To attain the highest level of integrity and security with regard to the investment assets and its managers
- To establish a cost of structuring and asset management economical to the size of investment

In essence, these can be summarized as follows:

(a) Confidentiality

(b) Integrity

(c) Security

(d) Economy

Parameters

- Aversion to venture capital situations and non-institutional investments, with preservation of capital being a priority
- Acceptance of and eagerness to grasp international investment opportunities and to globalize their investment horizon
- Long-term investment philosophy founded in professionally managed funds of reputable fund managers
- US$100,000 or more to invest

In summary, the parameters are:

(a) Risk aversion

(b) Medium to high net worth

(c) Internationally oriented

(d) Long-term investment view

Obstacles to Establishing Goals and Objectives

The investor as defined above faces serious problems in attempting to maximize his requirements. To my mind, these are as follows:

1. Too many professionals who only structure

These professional advisors position themselves firmly and squarely in the confidentiality business and little else. For $20,000 or more the client will get an elaborate structure with high ongoing costs. Please understand that I am not knocking the need for this. However, for the majority of clients in the defined segment, these structures are overkill, and as a result, overpriced. Also, once in possession of the structure, the client often doesn't know what to do with it from an investment standpoint. I call this the law of 99/1 (99% structuring, 1% investment).

2. Too many institutions that don't care about the structuring

Too many fatal errors are incurred by equating numbered bank accounts, for example, with confidentiality. Let me make the following statements on this subject:

(a) A numbered account is a personal account, supplemented by signatures, addresses, passport copies, and so on. The bank states that because it is numbered and/or coded, the client's name can be left out of focus. Therefore, the account is confidential and secret. This is simply not true; whichever way you cut it, the bank knows who you are.

(b) The business of banks is to promote investment, not secrecy. As much as secrecy is promised in efforts to promote banking services, the two forces are counter-cyclical. As the bank's growth in investment services grows and strengthens, thus necessitating increased staffing, paperflow and delegation, its ability to maintain secrecy and confidentiality wanes. If you accept the statement above —I repeat, whichever way you cut it, the bank knows who you are — this is not a comforting thought.

(c) Structuring a trust or offshore company on their own, or even together, doesn't help most of the time. Why? Simply because the major banks today are required to know who is underneath the trust, that is, who are the beneficiaries and settlor (founder) of the trust, or who are the beneficial shareholders of the company.

(d) The bank's paranoia in this regard — quite rightly I might add — arises from illicit drug traders and money launderers using these vehicles as confidential channels of investment. Unfortunately, the system does not differentiate between legitimate seekers of secrecy from the illegitimate. The net result: your confidentiality is compromised.

(e) This I call the 1/99 law (1% structuring, 99% investment)

3. Remoteness, the Unknown and Fear

A common myth: "Offshore locations are thousands of miles from the investor's country of residence, on islands never heard of (essentially banana republics). If the sharks don't grab your money, the tinpot dictator of the island eventually will." If you believe this you would be deservedly very afraid. As you will see, this is not a factual notion at all.

Achieving Goals and Meeting Parameters for the Defined Segment

As a professional consultant in the international arena, I have researched a vast array of structuring alternatives and investment options. To avoid boring the reader with a detailed analysis, I will cut right to the chase: Our selections for the defined segment are as follows:

- Offshore location for investment of assets — Isle of Man
- Registration of client's offshore discretionary trust — Jersey
- Institutional fund managers — life insurance institutions (LIs)
- Recommended trustees — corporate trust companies who have passed exacting due diligence requirements; never individuals or companies without fidelity insurance coverage.

I will focus on each of these aspects separately.

1. Why the Isle of Man (IM) and Jersey?
Consider the following:

Stability

IM represents not only the oldest continuous parliament in the world, it is also free from party politics. It has its own courts, but its law is based on English common law. Jersey represents similar characteristics of stability.

Legally Sound

(a) IM and Jersey were granted Designated Territory Status, Section 130, Financial Services Act 1986. United Kingdom investor-protection laws rank as some of the strictest in the world. The U.K. Department of Trade and Industry will only grant designated status where it is satisfied that a legislative framework offers as high a degree of investor protection as the U.K. itself.

(b) Most of the civil law legislation is modeled on United Kingdom Acts of Parliament. This means that the Isle of Man and Jersey legislation is at least as comprehensive as the U.K.

Security and Peace of Mind

As stated above, life insurance companies are the primary investment institutions we recommend. The Isle of Man Assurance (Compensation of Policyholders) Regulations, 1991, provide a high level of protection for those holding policies issued by Isle of Man–based life assurance companies. Brief details are as follows:

(a) Policy holders anywhere in the world are protected against default of the institution (should it occur) for 90% of the policy value.

(b) There is no upper limit attached to this value.

(c) To be a registered institution in IM, conformity to protection regulations is a prerequisite.

Tax Havens
Non-resident investors do not have any liabilities to Isle of Man or Jersey tax on the income or capital gains of their investment funds.

Trust Legislation
Jersey and Isle of Man have established exceptional company and trust legal systems to assist investors in attaining the highest levels of confidentiality.

2. Some important questions and answers regarding life insurance institutions (LIs)

Q. Do LIs, combined with an appropriately structured trust, close the confidentiality gaps in the investment structure?
A.   Absolutely. This can be established through the full channel of investment by structuring life insurance investment contracts.

Q. Does this mean you lose flexibility and compromise on security?
A. Absolutely not. LI contracts can be affected without hampering the client's flexibility and enhance the security of the investment if established in the right jurisdiction.

Q. Aside from the integrity of the jurisdiction, and protection offered to investors by legislation, how strong are the LIs themselves?
A. In most cases at least an AA rating by Standard and Poor. Very significant assets under management (per company assets under management ranging from US$11 billion to $280 billion). Reputed pension providers with historical performance dating back over 100 years.

Q. How wide is the range of investment choice?
A. Practically unlimited. Access to the world's foremost fund managers through the established structures is a meaningful feature of the alternatives offered.

Q. Is there a premium charged by the LIs for death benefit?
A   Only if specially required. In all other cases these are LI investment contracts which

pay out on maturity of the investment. Under these circumstances there is no extra cost for the policies.

Q. *Who, then, is the beneficiary, and whose lives are insured?*
A. The beneficiary is the trust. The lives insured are those of the trustees of the corporate trust company

Q. *How good are the reputations of the LIs as fund managers?*
A. We only recommend U.K. fund managers with stellar performances and outstanding reputations in their specialized fields. There is no one company which is positioned to offer everything to everyone. In all cases, we deal with their Isle of Man subsidiary.

3. Some important questions and answers regarding trusts in Jersey

Q. *Can I set up a trust without it being known that I am the settlor?*
A. Yes.

Q. *If I put money into a trust, can I draw an income from the trust during my lifetime, or get some of my capital back should I require it?*
A. Yes.

Q. *Can I arrange for other members of my family (or certain friends) to be financially provided for by the trustees after my death?*
A. Yes.

Q *After I have created the trust can I continue to manage the trust investments?*
A. Yes; the trustees have the power to delegate this to an approved investment advisor — who may, indeed, be yourself.

Q. *Can I own my own trust company, or even be a co-trustee myself?*
A. No.

Q. *If I set up a trust, do I lose control of my assets?*
A. The result of setting up a trust is that you cease to be the legal owner of the assets placed in trust. This, however, does not mean you divest yourself of control. As long as wishes expressed by trustors are for benefit of beneficiaries and are legal, they will be obeyed.

Q. *Can my trust own assets in several different countries?*
A. Yes. However, passing to the trustee the title to certain assets, such as real property, can cause difficulties in a few countries, and we would recommend that you seek advice from a specialist in this matter.

Q. *Do I have to decide now who the beneficiaries are and to how much they are entitled?*
A. No. With a discretionary trust, you can change your letter of wishes at any time.

Q. *Can I influence the decision?*
A. Yes, by writing what is called a "letter of wishes" for trustees to follow.

Q. *Can I change my letter of wishes?*
A. Yes, as often as you like, provided you do not contradict the terms of the trust deed.

Q. *How safe are my assets from misappropriation or misuse by the trustees or in the event of the bankruptcy of the trustees?*
A. Trust companies can only be formed in Jersey if the owners and management are of unimpeachable reputation and satisfy the Jersey authorities in this respect. For example, a company we recommend has six directors, and was established in 1976 with offices in London, Jersey, Cayman Islands, Liechtenstein and Switzerland. Each director carries fidelity insurance of one million pounds sterling per client per claim. Their clients come from all corners of the world and assets entrusted to them run into billions of dollars.

Other Advisors

It is not the goal of a responsible international investment advisor to recommend strategies that may be construed as tax evasion. Accordingly, any consultant positioning himself in the international arena should be comfortable working alongside the client's conventional professional advisors to reach an optimal solution.

A FINAL NOTE

This is by no means an exhaustive exposure of international investments and structuring. It is, however, an attempt to clear up misconceptions often associated with this arena. It also provides a framework for utilizing the various mechanisms reliably and in the correct context.

Chapter 9

Living Your Estate Plan Today: The Snowbird Lifestyle

— Brian Koscak, J.D., L.L.B., CSA, and Mark Simone, Medipac Int.—

Many Canadians who are planning to retire or who have already retired are opting to become snowbirds. Snowbirds are Canadian residents who escape our harsh winters and spend anywhere from one to six months a year at sunny destinations around the world. Popular Canadian snowbird winter destinations in the United States include Florida, Arizona, Texas and California.

As the Baby Boomers begin to reach retirement age, increasing numbers will be looking for sunnier and warmer climates for health-related reasons or to enjoy a preferred lifestyle. For example, many Canadians with respiratory problems or arthritis prefer Arizona's dry air and desert climate because for some it results in reduced health-related problems.

Snowbirds usually own or rent two properties, one in Canada and one in the United States. This transient lifestyle allows Canadians to enjoy the best of two great countries while retaining the rights and privileges of Canadian citizenship.

An increasing number of Canadians who are retired or semiretired are also looking for alternative lifestyles. Many are selling their primary Canadian residence and living at their cottage during the summer and fall, and then travelling to their U.S. property for winter and spring. Although snowbirds have been traditionally associated with the elderly, many aging Baby Boomers are adopting this preferred lifestyle as they get older and find their values changing.

Who is a Snowbird? Key Statistics

1. Age

Average age	66.3 years
Under age 65	25%
Between ages 65–74	60%
Over age 74	15%

2. Financial

Retired	90%
Average annual family income	C$41,200
Percent who receive a government pension	90%
Percent who have a private pension	60%
Percent who receive investment income	66%

3. Habitational Arrangements

Percent who own their Canadian residence	84%
Percent who own their American residence	75%
Types of American residences owned:	
• motor home, mobile home or trailer	30%
• condominium	25%
• houses	17%
• other	28%

4. Miscellaneous

Married	81%
Most popular month of departure	November
Percent who drive to their American winter destination	82%
Percent who fly to their American winter destination	10%
Average stay out of country	3.5 months
Percent of snowbirds who receive family visitors at their American winter residence once a year	42%

Why Are Canadian Winter Retirees Called Snowbirds?

Canadian snowbirds have always been closely identified with the annual migration of the Canadian geese to southern warmer climates upon the onset of the fall and winter seasons. The geese fly in their famous "V" pattern because it allows the group to fly farther and with less energy. For example, each bird in the V formation provides an updraft for the one behind, and in so doing, the flock can fly 71% farther and with less energy. In addition, when one goose gets sick or falls behind, at least two others break the formation to help their fellow goose.

The Canadian Snowbird Association, by mimicking Mother Nature, similarly has banded together to protect and put forward the issues and concerns affecting all snowbirds across Canada. There is definitely strength in numbers!

What is the Canadian Snowbird Association?

The Canadian Snowbird Association, or CSA, was formed in the spring of 1992. It is a not-for-profit organization incorporated in Canada and serves the needs and concerns of its members.

The CSA has an elected board of directors representing each province of Canada. The association is completely funded by its membership and receives no government assistance. This independence is important since one of the primary mandates of the CSA is to influence and lobby government to defend and enhance snowbird rights.

How Did the CSA Get Started?

The CSA was born on March 19, 1992, in Lakeland, Florida, as a grass-roots protest movement to address provincial cutbacks in out-of-country medical benefits. Previously, the various provincial health insurance plans (i.e., Medicare) provided nearly full reimbursement for the costs of out-of-country medical services. However, government cutbacks to Medicare caused provincial politicians to significantly reduce out-of-country payments as an alleged unnecessary expenditure. In October 1991, when most snowbirds had already left Canada for their winter destination, the Ontario government drastically reduced out-of-country hospital benefits to $400 per day.

In response, snowbirds quickly formed their own organization to lobby government and to obtain a "group" travel insurance program for their members, thereby replacing their lost benefits. The collective response by snowbirds was immediate because the cost for private travel insurance literally doubled overnight.

In the early days, a core group of pioneer CSA directors, led by Art Jackson, Jack Parry, Don Slinger, Frank Oliver and Evelyn Goodings, volunteered their time and homes to get this fledgling organization off the ground. In the first few months of the organization's existence, they quickly assembled 25,000 paid members and sought an insurance intermediary to negotiate the best plan and rates for their members.

The CSA made numerous requests for proposals from the insurance industry, and after months of discussions negotiated the best deal with Medipac International Inc. — a Toronto insurance intermediary that specializes in out-of-country travel insurance.

Who is Medipac International Inc.?

Medipac International Inc. is an insurance intermediary that provides the CSA with its out-of-country travel medical insurance program. Medipac is a private corporation formed in 1983 and is part of the Reed Mather Insurance Group.

Medipac's primary function is to design the CSA insurance plan and find the most competitive underwriter. Medipac's staff exceeds 130 employees during peak season and operates an international call centre from its head office in Toronto.

Medipac International was also selected as the administrator of the CSA based on its experience with other large groups and associations. Medipac provides many services to the CSA including sales and marketing, office administration, telecommunications, automation support, lobby and government relations and publishing.

Medipac reports directly to the CSA board of directors who are elected and give their time on a volunteer basis. The CSA operates according to established bylaws and works with Medipac in a manner akin to an employer/employee relationship.

CSA — Founding Principles

The CSA was founded on five pillars of strength:

1. Membership Benefits

Part of the association's strength is its group purchasing power. The sheer number of identifiable snowbirds make this uniquely organized group a key market niche for corporations. Target marketing for companies translates into membership discounts which are discussed in the next sections.

2. Communications

The CSA places a tremendous importance on communication with its members. As a national organization, constant communication is the glue that keeps this association together. The CSA keeps in touch with its members in a number of ways, including the *CSA News* magazine; Snowbird Extravaganza; consumer trade shows; winter information meetings; radio programs and television specials.

3. Social Interaction

Let's face it, part of the reason to join the CSA is to have fun and join other like-minded individuals who share the same lifestyle and interests. At all CSA gatherings, the association does its best to provide enough fun, frolic and frivolity for everyone. It does this through quality entertainment and information seminars conducted in an open and friendly environment. All members and future members are always welcome.

4. Government Issues

A main part of the CSA focus is government lobby and communications. The CSA has a reputation as a powerful lobby group and has many successes including:

- residency requirements
- absentee voting rights
- out-of-country hospital payments; and
- other cross-border issues

5. Corporate Alliances

Lastly, the CSA has formed many alliance relationships with key corporations. These companies target snowbirds with their products and services, while offering group membership discounts. Moreover, the CSA often earns a nominal amount to help support itself and its many programs. A win-win-win situation for everyone.

What Are the Benefits of a CSA Membership?

When the CSA started in 1992, its main goals were insurance and defending the Canada Health Act. Two years later, in May 1994, the CSA initiated a Membership Benefits Program to provide greater value to CSA members.

As a not-for-profit organization, the CSA has found alternative means of raising revenue. Everybody wins with a Membership Benefits Program. The member receives a group discount, the company increases sales, and the association receives a nominal contribution based on performance. All this helps keep membership dues as low as possible.

Today, it costs $10 per person or $15 per family to join the CSA each year. In addition to receiving five issues of the *CSA News*, members can take advantage of the CSA's Membership Benefits Program. The table opposite briefly describes each membership benefit.

Membership Benefit	**Provider**
Out-of-Country Travel Insurance The Medipac Travel Insurance package is endorsed by the CSA and is automatically mailed to members each year, before the travel season begins.	Medipac International Inc. 1-800-563-5104
Financial Planning and Money Management Independent and objective advice from financial planners who can undertake a needs assessment and truly recommend the right investment vehicle.	Dundee Wealth Management
Currency Exchange Transfer your funds automatically every month from your Canadian bank account to your U.S. account at wholesale exchange rates.	CSA Currency Exchange 1-800-265-3200
Auto and Home Insurance Program Proper auto protection at home and while travelling in the United States.	CSA Auto/Home Insurance Plan 1-800-267-8000
Personal Accident Insurance A specially designed plan provides full 24-hour-a-day, 365-day-a-year protection against accidents anywhere in the world.	CSA Personal Accident Insurance 1-800-238-8953
Internet Service Exclusive cross-border pricing arrangements for CSA members. Keyword: Snowbird.	AOL Canada 1-800-265-3200
Golf Fees Free green fees for two rounds a year at each of more than 1,600 courses; up to 50% off green and cart fees at an additional 1,900 courses.	The Golf Card 1-800-513-7576
Auto Club You choose the tow vehicle and send in the claim. We guarantee payment within 30 busi- ness days.	CSA Auto Club 1-800-265-3200

For more information on the CSA, call or write:
Canadian Snowbird Association
180 Lesmill Road, North York, Ontario M3B 2T5 / 1-800-265-3200 / 416-391-9000

How Does the CSA Communicate with Its Members?

The CSA has its own magazine, aptly titled the *CSA News,* which is published five times a year. It is a colourful, easy-to-read magazine that focuses on snowbird-related issues. It is regularly mailed to members at their Canadian or international winter residence, depending on the time of year.

Snowbird Extravaganza

After the first annual general meeting in January 1993, the CSA, in conjunction with Medipac International, realized that it needed to talk to its members face to face, hence the creation of Snowbird Extravaganza. This event is an annual two-day consumer trade show held at the Florida State fairgrounds in Tampa, Florida. It caters to both Canadian and American winter residents and is billed as the largest gathering of Canadians annually, outside of World War II. In four short years, Snowbird Extravaganza has become such a huge success that in January 1997 it had in excess of 80,000 attendees. With over 350 corporate sponsors and two days of nonstop quality entertainment, it's amazing that this event is *absolutely free!*

The show has become so popular that *Macleans* magazine reported on the event in its February 10, 1997, weekly edition. The event is scheduled near the end of January and is a "must-see" attraction if you are in the area at this time.

Based on the success of Snowbird Extravaganza, the CSA and Medipac International have planned three additional shows or "mini extravaganzas" for Arizona, Texas and California. Moreover, the CSA and Medipac International have also launched "Extravaganza North" for Toronto.

Winter Information Meetings

Besides Snowbird Extravaganza, the CSA travels to many other snowbird winter destinations throughout the United States. The CSA undertakes annual winter information meetings in other parts of Florida, Texas, Arizona and California. These meetings allow the association to keep in touch with its members by combining entertainment, seminars and a miniconsumer show which caters to the snowbird lifestyle.

Right to Vote in Federal Elections while Out of Country

One of the founding objectives of the CSA was to obtain the right to vote while temporarily residing out of country during a federal election. A majority of CSA members travel during the fall when federal elections have often been called. The CSA successfully lobbied for amendments to the Canada Elections Act contained in Bill C-114 and proclaimed by parliament on May 6, 1993. The amendment permitted Canadian citizens to vote in a federal election, if they temporarily resided outside their riding or have been living abroad for less than five years.

Residency Issues: 183-Day Maximum — Prisoners in Our Own Province
The CSA has fought long and hard with all levels of government to eliminate or increase the number of months that snowbirds can remain out of province or country and still be eligible for government health insurance. Currently, all provinces, except Newfoundland, British Columbia and Quebec, allow their residents to remain out of country or province for no longer than 183 days in any 12-month period. Newfoundland allows its residents to remain out of country or province for up to 8 months in any 12-month calendar period. Although Quebec and British Columbia have the same 183-day limitation, they both allow for unlimited travel to other provinces up to a stipulated period of time.

Many snowbirds believe that such limitations on one's mobility rights render themselves "prisoners in their own province." For example, if an Albertan resides in Naples, Florida, for six months, upon their return they legally cannot travel to another province to visit their family and friends. Snowbirds, as taxpaying Canadians, believe that the 183-day limitation is a harsh restriction on their right to travel.

Therefore, the CSA is taking action to repeal the discriminatory 183-day residency rule. Although most snowbirds would undoubtedly prefer a longer stay out of country, such as eight months as in Newfoundland, the CSA believes the more pragmatic solution would be the "Quebec compromise." The Quebec compromise simply maintains the 183-day rule for out-of-country travel, but allows unlimited short-term trips within the country not exceeding a certain number of days.

If a person violates the 183-day rule and stays out of country longer than legally permissible and is caught, he or she could lose their provincial health coverage. Without underlying provincial health coverage, one could not purchase supplemental health insurance since it is a condition of purchase. Moreover, if you are caught, it takes three months to have your provincial health insurance reinstated.

Although the CSA is making inroads with the government in rethinking the 183-day residency rule, at one time the province of New Brunswick wanted to reduce it even further — to 90 days.

The Future of the Canada Health Act
The CSA has been a staunch defender of the Canada Health Act. Some may say that the association has a selfish interest in preserving the Act, since it promotes their interests. True. But the CSA's defence benefits all Canadians. If the federal government and provinces can break a clear legislative requirement of the Act without impunity, then what is to prevent them from attacking other fundamental principles of the Act. Simply, it is the domino effect, whereby one transgression will lead to another and soon we will be travelling down a slippery slope to the point of Americanizing or privatizing health care services in Canada.

Some may believe such reasoning is far fetched. Think again. In the summer of 1995, the prime minister held a first-minister meeting wherein the premiers again raised the spectre of a renegotiation of Medicare. The premiers simply wanted the federal money and the power to decide how to spend it. This type of provincial parochialism is what the Act was designed to prevent, which if allowed would result in a patch-quilt of health care services across Canada.

The letters the CSA has received from various provincial ministers of health simply state that the provinces cannot afford Medicare and are demanding its reform. Despite clear legislative wording, as found in the portability section, provinces are acting as if out-of-country payments can be reduced based on a government's decision to re-allocate money. In other words, provinces believe they can break the law and unilaterally defy the federal government.

Recently, the provinces of Alberta and Ontario began closing hospitals and asking the private sector to step in and operate for-profit facilities. In essence, the provinces seem bent on introducing user fees and a two-tier medical system, one for the rich and one for the poor.

Therefore, if you think that the CSA is being overly zealous or selfishly pursuing its own interest, then you are only half right. The CSA's defence of the Canada Health Act is just that — a defence of a legal right given by government and ignored by government. An erosion of even one right demands to be addressed, because if today it is health care, then tomorrow it will be your registered retirement savings plan. Think about it!

OUT-OF-COUNTRY TRAVEL INSURANCE IN A NUTSHELL

What Is a Government Health Insurance Plan?
A Government Health Insurance Plan (GHIP) is a government-funded insurance plan which covers residents of a certain province for specified health-related products and services. Each province has its own separate and distinct health insurance plan. Each provincial plan is jointly funded by the province and the federal government. However, to receive federal money, each province must comply with the requirements stipulated by the Canada Health Act.

What Is the Canada Health Act?
The Canada Health Act is federal legislation which provides for universal Medicare across Canada. It is what many believe uniquely distinguishes ourselves from the United States. As Canadians, we believe that as a matter of social policy, all citizens, regardless of income, have a right to certain standards of health care.

The five principles of Medicare enshrined in the Act include universality, portability, accessibility, comprehensiveness and open, public administration.

Despite the Act, governments, both federally and provincially, have been whittling away at GHIP as health care costs have escalated, especially with an aging population. The 1990s saw ever increasing or new user fees, hospital closures, delisting of drugs previously covered by provincial drug plans and reductions in out-of-country payments.

Successive governments have failed to enforce the Act by reducing health care expenditures, and politicians are accused of doublespeak. On the one hand, they want to pre-serve this vital piece of social legislation, yet on the other hand they are subtly attacking it. Their strategy is simple: Rather than killing the Act outright, it has become the death of a thousand cuts. However, all governments universally recommend that citizens buy pri-vate travel insurance when travelling out of country or province.

Why Buy Private Insurance?

Many health services outside Canada cost more than the amount covered by your provin-cial health insurance plan. You are liable for the difference in cost. Some expenses are not covered by the government and you will be required to pay the full costs, unless you have purchased private insurance. Take, for example, a resident of Ontario who has a heart attack in Florida.

Fees for 10 days of hospitalization	$	50,000
Amount reimbursed by Ontario Health Insurance Plan		4,000
Amount payable by patient	$	46,000

Note: figures are approximate for 1999

As the above example illustrates, the shortfall from the actual amounts billed by the hos-pital and paid by OHIP is $46,000. This amount must be paid by either the patient or his or her insurance company, if he or she purchased insurance.

Accidents can happen to anyone, at any time and at any place. They have occurred on weekend shopping trips to the United States or extended vacations to exotic destinations. Therefore, it is absolutely essential that you purchase out-of-country travel insurance before you leave your resident province.

"Going Bare" —Taking a Chance and Not Buying Insurance

Some snowbirds, when faced with increasing costs of private travel insurance, may consider not buying insurance. According to a CSA survey conducted in the summer of 1994, 6% of CSA members travelled without out-of-country travel insurance. In the industry, this is called "going bare." These risk-takers feel confident that they are in good health and are immune from an accident.

To those considering taking such a horrendous risk — don't do it! The risks to you and your family's personal health and financial well-being are simply too great. A day in some United States hospitals costs in excess of US$2,000. In an intensive care unit, the price is easily doubled. An illness requiring a prolonged stay can use up all your life savings.

Furthermore, without insurance, there is no third party with a vested, financial stake (your insurance company) that is interested in getting you stabilized and back home as soon as possible. In fact the opposite might happen.

However, the most important consideration is the possibility of delay if you don't have coverage. Trying to prove that you are able to pay for hospital services without insurance may slow down emergency care when you need it the fastest. One must remember that hospitals in the United States are businesses, and receiving medical attention is not a right as in Canada.

If you believe these comments seem like scare tactics, you are right. The CSA has heard about numerous examples of snowbirds caught in these circumstances which have literally bankrupted families.

If this doesn't convince you, consider the fact that every provincial government in Canada and the federal government recommends, in the strongest terms possible, that all Canadians purchase travel insurance whether they travel out of province or country. They too have seen the catastrophic results. The fact that provinces are to blame for the high cost of travel insurance is another story. However, if you cannot afford full coverage from a private insurance company, consider the following alternatives:

- Shorten the length of your stay. The shorter the stay, the lower the risk for insurance companies and the lower the rate.

- Find a catastrophic insurance policy where the deductible is $5,000 or $10,000. This sets a limit on your risk and can reduce your initial premium. If you cannot afford such high deductibles while travelling in the United States, consider obtaining a credit card that can be used to pay for the deductible in the event of an emergency. When an accident strikes, you do not have the time to determine how you will get the money to pay for the deductible.

- Don't go at all. It's a tough decision, one that governments and circumstances may have forced upon you. But in the wisest analysis, it may be the best course of action.

When it comes to out-of-country travel insurance protection, don't leave Canada without it!

Residency Requirements

Coverage under a provincial Government Health Insurance Plan requires that you have a valid provincial health insurance card. Residency is an important issue for snowbirds because it determines how long one can stay out of country and still have valid provincial health coverage. If you stay longer than legally allowed, then any claim incurred after such time could be denied.

Travelling Canadians should be aware that provincial out-of-country coverage is limited to a certain number of days. Currently, each province, except Newfoundland, Quebec, and British Columbia, requires a resident to remain in province for at least 183 days a year. Inversely, one cannot be out of your resident province in excess of six months a year.

Newfoundland is the only province that allows its residents to remain out of country or province for up to eight months in any twelve-month period.

British Columbia and Quebec also have the 183-day residency rule; however, they allow unlimited short-term travel in excess of 183 days. Quebec allows short-term trips up to 21 days outside Quebec, meaning out of province or country, and these trips are not included in the calculation of 183 days in a calendar year. Moreover, Quebec allows stays out of country for up to 12 months, once every 7 years, upon application to the Regie d'assurance. British Columbia only allows short-term trips in excess of 183 days (but only out of province, not country) for a stipulated period of time.

Many snowbirds who stay out of country for six months believe that it is unfair that they cannot visit family in other provinces without the risk of having their insurance revoked. These individuals have paid their taxes all their lives and resent restrictions on their mobility rights during their retirement years.

Exceeding the Residency Requirements
Some people believe that they don't need to worry about the 183-day residency rule. These daring individuals assume that the bureaucrats at their provincial ministry of health won't catch them because they have no way of monitoring when people depart and enter Canada or travel to other provinces.

It is true that the ministries of health do not have extensive systems that monitor when one exits or enters the country or another province. However, if you are found to have exceeded your provincial residency rule, then in addition to having your claim denied, you risk losing your entire health care coverage. You will now have to wait approximately 90 days until your coverage may be reinstated.

In summary, snowbirds should not play Russian roulette with their health care, especially seniors who have a greater chance of getting sick, when it can easily be avoided by obeying the law.

Final Helpful Hints Prior to Departure

- In a medical emergency, phone your Emergency Assistance Hotline number immediately. They can direct you to the proper facilities, coordinate payment, and help with other issues.

- Carry both your provincial health insurance card and private travel insurance card with you at all times.

- Remember, your insurance plan is for medical emergencies only. Before leaving Canada, stock up on your medication or any other health needs. Make sure both the birth date and provincial health care number are provided for the same person. About one-third of all claims are delayed because these numbers do not match.

- Always get original receipts and bills and keep photocopies for your records. No insurance plan accepts copies.

- Lastly, to speed up claims processing, include a photocopy of your provincial health insurance card and private travel insurance card with your claims documentation.

OTHER OUT-OF-COUNTRY TRAVEL INSURANCE ISSUES

Out-of-Country/Out-of-Province Travel Insurance — What Is the Difference?

Many people believe that they only need travel health insurance when they travel outside the country. Not true! You may also need it when you travel outside your resident province. Despite the existence of the Canada Health Act, each provincial health insurance plan lists specified products and services it covers, including maximum dollar amounts, limitations and exclusions. Therefore, you may find that a cost that is covered in one province is excluded or partially covered in another province. The total or partial difference in costs will be paid by you, despite requiring these emergency services within your own country. All charges for excess services can be insured while you travel in another province.

For example, in 1992 the CSA became aware of a Manitoba woman who was visiting relatives in a small town north of Edmonton. She suffered a heart attack and had to be moved to an Edmonton hospital by air ambulance. The cost was $5,000. However, she had to pay the entire cost of air ambulance transportation back to her home province because Manitoba's health insurance plan excluded these services. Canadians travelling outside their home province cannot afford to take anything for granted in terms of medical insurance coverage.

As a general rule, always consult your insurance broker when travelling out of province or country. For more information call Medipac International at 1-800-563-5104.

How Are Claims Paid for Services Provided in Another Province?

For the most part, claims for medically required physician and hospital services received in a Canadian province or territory (except Quebec) are billed automatically through the provincial medical plans. All provinces, except Quebec, participate in a similar hospital reciprocal agreement. Quebec has an agreement with hospitals but not with physicians. This means that a Quebec resident, or anyone travelling in Quebec who is not a resident, may be asked to pay upfront for payment and later get reimbursed by their provincial health plan in the absence of private travel insurance.

Make sure that you present your personal health card when medical reimbursable services are required, otherwise you may be responsible for payment at the time of service. Although you may be reimbursed later by your resident province, such an out-of-pocket expense — which may involve significant amounts of money and delay — can be avoided.

When Do Snowbirds Typically Buy Out-of-Country Travel Insurance?

In 1992, most snowbirds bought out-of-country travel medical insurance when they departed for their winter destination. However, departure dates and purchasing decisions have changed over the years, just as the market has changed.

In 1992, most snowbirds made their purchasing decisions after the September Labour Day weekend and the bulk of snowbirds departed in the month of October. Today, with more insurance companies in the marketplace, purchasing inquiries are made any time from June onward as insurance companies release their rates and policies for the upcoming season. In fact, as insurance companies jockey for position to get market share, snowbirds often see discounts in rates. Rate reductions and underwriting restrictions after rate releases have become common in the industry as insurance companies compete with one another for snowbird insurance dollars.

According to statistics supplied by Medipac International, most snowbirds now depart in November and have shortened their stays out of country. In 1992, the average snowbird season was five months, today it is three and a half months. Government cutbacks to out-of-country payments across Canada have increased travel insurance premiums and many snowbirds on fixed incomes simply cannot afford the extra cost for both spouses.

Why Don't Insurance Companies Offer One Price for All Snowbirds?
Travel insurance is a very competitive market, with over 100 companies competing for your insurance dollar. Some snowbirds believe that everyone should pay the same price, regardless of age, sex or other risk-determining factors. The benefit of such an approach is that everyone pays a fixed cost based on the averages of both higher- and lower-risk travellers. This approach is similar to the level paying premium approach adopted by the group insurance industry. When you pay a flat amount, you are really paying a higher premium when you are young and healthier and a lower premium when you are older and no longer in good health. The averaged flat amount ensures a fixed and affordable premium throughout one's policy instead of charging higher rates when you are older or less healthy and less able to afford them.

Although level travel insurance premiums are a good idea in theory, they simply won't work in practice. Rather than dealing with an individual over his or her lifetime, we are dealing with a group of people largely over the age of 65. Healthier snowbirds want to pay the lowest price possible and will not pay to subsidize unhealthy or higher-risk snowbirds. They will only pay the rate commensurate with the risk.

Moreover, if the CSA adopted a level-paying premium scheme for snowbirds, it would inevitably price itself out of the market. Healthier snowbirds would be less inclined to buy the policy since they undoubtedly could obtain similar coverage cheaper elsewhere. That leaves a snowbird plan with those who are less healthy which will produce higher-than-average claims for the group. This means that the insurance company will be forced to pay out more claims than premiums collected, which could financially destroy the plan.

Despite the cry for government-run insurance, especially in auto insurance, travel insurance is still one of the most competitive industries in Canada where insurance companies annually compete for your hard-earned dollars.

Why Do Travel Insurance Rates Go Up Every Year?

Travel insurance is no different from other insurance. Simply, the premiums of the many pay for the losses of a few. However, when premiums collected are insufficient to pay claims incurred, then an insurance company sustains losses. The new rates will undoubtedly be higher than the previous year's rates, not because an insurance company is trying to recoup its losses, rather the rates accurately reflect the claims experience of the group. This means that the rates or premiums collected reflect an adequate amount of money an insurance company believes is necessary to pay for future claims and its expenses of running the plan.

In the early 1990s, premiums skyrocketed for five reasons: one, provincial governments reduced the amount they would pay for out-of-country expenses; two, hospitals in the United States charged foreign visitors excessive prices and sometimes for unnecessary tests and procedures; three, radical fluctuations in the Canadian dollar; four, inefficient claims-processing procedures; and five, a high frequency of low-dollar claims.

Since the mid-1990s, the travel insurance business has been overhauled. The industry has successfully addressed the overcharging practices by United States hospitals by setting up managed care systems and preferred-provider organizations. These early-warning intervention systems allow an insurance company to get involved in the claims management process as soon as possible. The insurance company works with hospital staff to ensure that only medically necessary treatment is provided.

Claims processing procedures have been improved and policy contracts have been worded to eliminate low-dollar nuisance claims that can be more easily absorbed by the patient. Moreover, many insurance companies have instituted cost-containment measures such as co-insurance or deductible features within their policy to ensure that it is principally used for major or catastrophic losses.

What Is Managed Care?

Managed care consists of a rapid response to a medical emergency and the monitoring of care and follow-up. A company such as Medipac International and its underwriter are involved from the very first call, from helping the client find the appropriate medical facility or practitioner to diagnosis, treatment, evacuation (if necessary) and follow-up.

Most insurance companies have a toll-free 1-800 travel assistance hotline that an insured can call if medical treatment is required. If it is an emergency, always call the emergency response phone number in your area, usually 911, and then call the travel assistance hotline.

Be sure you make the call within a timely basis, i.e., at least within 24 hours, because travel insurance companies want to intervene as soon as possible to ensure proper and efficient treatment. They want to make sure that an overzealous hospital will not take out your appendix, for example, when all you have is a mild form of food poisoning. Some policies even make such phone calls within a certain timeframe mandatory, so read your policy carefully.

Once the call is made it is received by a response team whose job is to help during the emergency. Companies such as Medipac International and their underwriter have a travel assistance hotline that is answered by trained nurses. These trained professionals work with personnel at the admitting facility and make sure you get the right treatment as quickly as possible. They take details about you, assess the problem, confirm valid medical coverage, answer questions and recommend a nearby treatment facility. Medipac International even goes the extra mile by contacting family and friends back home, with the patient's permission. In summary, Medipac International ensures that your experience is professional and reliable, despite being an emergency.

Make sure that you always carry your travel assistance card provided by your travel insurance company. Not only does it have the name of your insurance company and policy number, it also has important numbers to call in the event of an emergency. When travelling abroad, never be without proper identification or your travel assistance card.

Can You "Top Up" Existing Insurance (Gold Credit Cards) by Purchasing Other Insurance?

In the early 1990s, many credit cards offered free travel health insurance from 21 to 60 days, as a value-added benefit attached to the card. However, as the industry changed and the government reduced the amount that it would pay for an out-of-country claim, many credit card companies stopped offering the benefit or reduced coverage to only a few weeks.

When such coverage was more prevalent and extensive, many travellers would purchase private travel insurance in addition to the coverage provided by their credit card. Simply, travellers would "top up" their credit card coverage by buying private travel insurance for the balance of their trip.

It is highly recommended that you read the insurance agreement provided by your credit card company. Many credit card travel insurance agreements have restrictions, limitations, exclusions and pre-existing conditions that require you to read the policy before leaving to ensure proper coverage.

For example, some gold credit cards only provide out-of-country coverage to age 65, thereby rendering such coverage useless for most snowbirds. Moreover some credit card companies expressly prohibit you from purchasing excess travel insurance on top of their base coverage. In the event of a loss, your claim may be void if your trip is longer than the number of days provided.

As a general rule, you are best to purchase travel insurance from the first day of your departure if you plan on staying out of country in excess of a few weeks.

Retirement Plans and Private Travel Insurance

Some employers have provided their employees with retirement packages that include out-of-country travel protection for a certain number of days. For example, most federal government superannuate plans provide coverage for the first 40 days of your trip outside Canada to a maximum of $100,000. Many retirees want to integrate such coverage with their private travel insurance company so they pay an overall lower premium. This is similar to a top-up which was previously discussed using credit cards.

Although integrating such plans makes sense because you may save money, make sure that your private travel insurance company allows such plan integration. Always make sure you read all your insurance literature.

Many retirement plans have a lifetime maximum. This is the maximum amount of claims that a plan will incur during a retiree's lifetime. For example, a plan with a $50,000 lifetime maximum gives a retiree a sum of money from which eligible claims, such as drug bills, will be deducted. Coverage ceases once the lifetime maximum is exhausted.

Some retirees are concerned that their travel insurance company may try to claim against their retirement plan before paying the balance of a claim, if necessary. Some private travel insurance contracts state that their coverage is secondary to any other available coverage. This means that in the event of a claim for $60,000, to carry on with the above example, your lifetime maximum would be instantly reduced, leaving the travel insurance company paying the balance. You now have nothing left for the remainder of your retirement.

Retirees should be aware of policies that do not protect their lifetime maximum. Therefore, if you have such a plan, make sure the insurance policy provides primary protection and specifically states that it will limit or exclude claims against a retirement plan.

Some retirees have used their retiree plan to reduce their travel insurance premiums by purchasing plans that offer higher deductibles. The higher the deductible, the lower your premium.

Canadian insurance guidelines suggest that retirement plans should not be reduced below $50,000 of their lifetime maximum for travel insurance claims. Although most insurance companies abide by the guideline, some don't which leaves you financially vulnerable.

For example, if you purchase a $5,000 deductible and have a $50,000 lifetime maximum provided by your retirement plan, then in the event of a claim, you may elect to charge the $5,000 against your retirement plan. Assuming no other deductions, you now would have a balance of $45,000 on your lifetime maximum with any excess amount of your claim paid by your private travel insurance company.

What to Look for When You Buy Travel Insurance

Disease Lists
Some plans do not cover all possible emergencies, rather only list emergencies or named perils. If you have a covered claim, then arguably you are lucky. It is preferable to buy an all-risk policy that covers most types of emergencies, subject to conditions, limitations or deductibles. As a general rule, avoid named peril or disease list policies.

Pre-Existing Conditions
A pre-existing condition is a medical condition that existed prior to your purchase of insurance. Most, if not all policies have pre-existing clauses or restrictions. For example, if you have a gastric ulcer that is controlled by medication and diet and it has been

flaring up before you leave for your trip out of country, then any expense related to this condition may not be covered in the event of a claim. The reason is simple. To cover such losses would be tantamount to insuring a burning house. Insurers cover risks of loss, not certainties or near certainties of loss. An ulcer, if not under control according to the above example, is akin to a burning house.

Read your insurance policy carefully, because a pre-existing medical clause may exclude or limit coverage. For example, many policies may exclude coverage if you had a heart attack or stroke in the last 12 months.

Co-Insurance
Co-insurance is a feature in which the insured must pay part of each claim. It is different from a deductible, which applies usually only once during a policy term. Co-insurance means the sharing of the insurance risk with your insurer, usually according to a stated percentage. For example, a policy with an 80% co-insurance clause requires you to pay 20% of a claim, with the insurer paying the balance. Although co-insurance clauses may result in lower premiums, the savings may simply be outweighed by the financial risk. Specifically, if a claim is $100,000 and the policy has a 80% co-insurance clause, then you must be prepared to pay $20,000, your share of the claim.

Deductibles
A deductible is a fixed amount that an insured must pay in the event of a claim. For example, a policy with a $500 deductible requires the insured to pay the first $500 of a claim, with the insurer paying the balance. If this same policy had a co-insurance clause, then not only would the insured be required to pay the deductible, but also their co-insurance percentage. Most policy deductibles are per trip for all claims, but some are deductibles per claim. Read your policy carefully.

Beware of what some plans call "disappearing deductibles." These plans sometimes require you to pay a deductible and sometimes they don't. A deductible may be waived or disappear upon the happening of a stated event or achievement of a certain claims threshold. For example, some policies may waive a deductible if you are admitted to a hospital as an in-patient, yet impose a deductible for out-patient services. Moreover, some policies require the payment of a deductible if a claim is under a certain dollar value, and waive it if it exceeds this amount. The end result is often confusion.

Low-Plan Limits
This one is truly dangerous. Each plan has a maximum limit on the amount of money they will pay in the event of a claim. Some plans have limitations of $50,000, which can be grossly inadequate. For example, the treatment for a heart attack in the United States can easily cost hundreds of thousands of dollars.

For example, a plan with a $100,000 limitation will require you to pay the balance in the event of a $200,000 claim. Therefore, although people may believe they have coverage, they may be in for a surprise if their coverage turns out to be grossly inadequate.

Hospital Restrictions

Managed care has come a long way since the early 1990s, but some managed care plans restrict your coverage to only certain hospitals. Therefore, when an emergency strikes, both you and your ambulance driver must know where to go to ensure you are covered. Going to the wrong hospital may result in denied insurance, which may aggravate your illness. Be especially concerned when dealing with these plans.

Hospital Deductibles

Hospital deductibles require you to pay for your first night in a hospital while the insurer pays the balance. This may seem inexpensive, but consider that the greatest expenses are incurred when you are first admitted, so, such a plan can be like having a large deductible. On one claim a patient incurred *$72,000* in six hours after having a heart attack.

No Direct Claims Payment

Direct claims payment is where the hospital bills your insurance company directly. The insurer later recoups any amount covered by your provincial health insurance plan. Plans that have no direct claims payment require you to pay the money upfront and then submit a claim. Be prepared to get a bank loan and then wait for your money some time in the future. Many of us could not get a loan for $10,000, let alone $1,000,000.

Claims in Canadian Dollars

Look for a policy with a U.S. dollar limit. Most claims are payable in U.S. dollars. Therefore, with a 50% exchange rate, your $1,000,000 policy limit really approximates $667,000, possibly resulting in underinsurance.

Area Surcharges

Some insurance companies cover a basic amount in all areas, but impose a surcharge for high-risk areas. Essentially, you may be out of pocket for the amount of the surcharge, if you have an emergency in a surcharged area. Realizing that most snowbirds drive to their winter residence and cannot anticipate an emergency, purchasers of these plans often do so at their own peril.

Price

Although price is an important factor when buying travel insurance, so is coverage, reputation and service. Chances are that if a price is too good to be true, it is. Prices reflect coverage, and chances are where a price is exceptionally inexpensive, it probably means that your coverage has been negatively affected. Read your policy carefully. It is always safer and preferable to purchase insurance from a known and reputable company.

Trip Interruptions

Some travel insurance plans allow you to interrupt your trip and return home for Christmas, thereby splitting your trip into two parts. Insurance industry parlance refers to these as "shuttle plans" or "multiple trip plans." These plans allow you to take two or more trips under the same insurance policy. The price you pay is based on the length of the longest trip. An interrupter plan issues only one policy and your price is based on the total number of days you are away.

At face value, they seem like a good idea, but there are potentially three main problems. First, some plans allow their pre-existing condition clause to start over again each time you leave Canada.

Second, you must leave from your province of residence to be automatically covered. For example, a person who lives in Ontario, travels through the United States to British Columbia, and later departs for Arizona would not be covered for the second part of his or her trip. Simply, he or she did not depart from Ontario, his or her originating province of departure.

And third, some plans require that you supply sufficient proof of your exit and re-entry into the country or call them before every departure — potential hassles and possibly lost information abound.

The solutions for this type of problem are twofold: (1) buy a separate policy for each trip and pay careful attention to any pre-existing condition clauses; and (2) buy one policy that covers you for everything, including your trip home for Christmas. You will probably pay for a few extra days, and you may have no reporting requirements, to worry about. Review these types of policies, and in particular any clause that may limit coverage for recurring conditions.

Medical Evacuations Due to Emergency Illness

Many snowbirds have unanswered questions in the event that they or their spouse are evacuated back to Canada due to a medical emergency. How do they get home? What about their spouse? Are they allowed to return to the United States? Is their travel insurance still valid after their emergency? How can they go home when their cottage is not winterized? These are some of the commonly asked questions.

The CSA has heard of situations where people were put on a plane, returned to their home city or town, and left on their own waiting for assistance which never came. One group believed its obligations ended at the airport runway. Make sure you talk to your travel insurance company about how this process works so you know exactly what will happen in the event of an emergency.

Medipac International and its travel insurance underwriter are a good example of what to do right. They suggest three ways that an evacuation can be handled:

1. If the patient's health has been stabilized, then provide the person and his or her spouse with a plane ticket, and send them home on the next available commercial airline. If necessary, provide a medical escort.

2. Section off an area for stretchers on a commercial airline;

3. Charter a specially equipped medical aircraft, often a Lear jet. Depending

on the circumstances, up to four doctors with a nursing team may accompany an evacuation to deal with any problems that may arise.

Medipac International and its travel insurance underwriter may utilize both doctors and a nursing team to ensure that a patient is sufficiently stabilized for air travel. Medipac then ensures that arrangements have been made upon arrival for the patient's family physician or specialist to meet them at the hospital and take over from there.

Medipac is one of the few travel insurance companies that pays to have a spouse fly back with the patient (or separately if no space is available on the air ambulance).

How Do You Submit a Claim?
If you have a claim, then submit your information to your private health insurance company directly. The insurance company usually pays eligible claims in full and seeks reimbursement afterwards from your provincial health insurance plan.

However, if your province of residence requires submission to the provincial plan first or if you have no private travel insurance, then send your information to your provincial ministry of health. When submitting a claim to the ministry of health, send the following information:

- details of treatment
- your original receipt for payment
- your name and current address
- your health number

To avoid delays, send your information as soon as possible, since many provinces will only accept claims anywhere from 6 to 12 months after the claim is incurred.

SNOWBIRD ISSUES PRIOR TO GOING SOUTH
There are a number of issues that snowbirds must consider prior to departing to their winter residence, including auto insurance, home insurance, mail forwarding, suspension of local telephone service, prescription drugs, passports and citizenship cards.

Auto Insurance and Driving to the United States
Many snowbirds drive their automobiles to their winter residence for extended periods of time. An auto insurance policy typically provides coverage anywhere in Canada and the United States. Recently, however, insurance companies have been surcharging snowbirds for this increased exposure to risk of loss. Some snowbirds are confused because the policy explicitly provides coverage in the United States, yet insurance companies want more money for the added risk.

A basic principle of insurance is that a premium is charged commensurate with the risk.

Insurers are arguing that coverage in the United States is based on occasional visits, not long-term stays. The longer the visit, the greater the risk. Moreover, currency conversion costs have justified some auto policy surcharges as high as 50%.

Some snowbirds may be inclined to withhold this information from their insurer and take their chances. However, if you fail to disclose, you may breach a policy requirement of reporting all material changes in risk. Long-term stays in the United States arguably are a material change in risk.

The number of days that you are out of country determine whether you will be surcharged. For example, most insurance companies will not surcharge you if you drive through the United States on a three-week vacation. However, as a general rule, contact your insurance broker for any trips in excess of three weeks.

When you return from your trip, call your insurance broker and immediately cancel the endorsement that surcharges you for travelling with your car in the United States. The surcharge is quoted on an annual basis and you should only pay for the added risk that you pose when you are in fact out of country.

Home Insurance

Many snowbirds have dual residences in Canada and the United States. Make sure that you have adequate coverage in both jurisdictions.

Prior to departing, make sure that you have made arrangements with family or friends to visit your dwelling to prevent or report any damage on a regular basis. Your dwelling policy has explicit procedures to follow prior to departing to the United States. Failure to abide by the procedures may result in the denial of coverage.

Specifically, most dwelling policies require you to have someone check on your premises at least once every four days if your unit is heated during the "usual heating season" or winter. Failure to abide by this provision may result in the denial of a claim caused by the freezing of a plumbing, heating, sprinkler, air conditioning system or domestic appliance.

However, you would be covered if you had arranged for a competent person to enter your dwelling or unit daily to ensure that the heating was being maintained; or if you had shut off the water supply and had drained all the pipes and appliances prior to departure.

If you rent your dwelling during your absence, always make sure that your tenant has sufficient and adequate insurance. In fact, request a copy of his or her certificate of insurance as a matter of record. Many dwelling policies exclude coverage resulting from vandalism or malicious acts caused by tenants or guests of tenants. This peril, however, is covered under a tenant's insurance policy.

As a general rule, always consult your local insurance broker for the correct procedures to follow to ensure that you have valid home insurance prior to your departure.

Mail Forward

Prior to departing to their winter destinations, snowbirds are advised to contact Canada Post and have their mail temporarily re-directed to the United States. Alternatively, it is advisable to have a member of your family or friend regularly pick up your mail and generally check up on your dwelling to ensure that everything is in order.

To effect a temporary re-direction of your mail, simply visit your local Canada Post station or outlet and ask for a temporary re-direction form. Complete the form and bring at least one piece of personal identification, like your driver's licence or birth certificate. Canada Post charges a fee to re-direct your mail and it is best to check the cost at your time of departure, since rates are subject to change.

Prior to returning to Canada, it is also advisable to contact the U.S. Postal Service and similarly have your mail re-directed back to Canada. Currently, there is no charge for this equivalent service in the United States.

Suspend Your Phone Service

Make sure that prior to your departure you temporarily suspend your local phone service, rather than paying full charges when you're not at home. Suspending your phone service has a number of advantages:

- protects against long-distance fraud and other unwanted charges, since there will be no incoming or outgoing calls;

- maintains your telephone number and directory listing;

- allows customers to continue to use their calling card, pay their long-distance bills, and maintain any savings plans; and

- forwards bills to a proper temporary address

As a suggestion, call you local phone company to investigate such a service and save money.

Taking Prescription Drugs Across the Border

Some snowbirds regularly take prescribed medication. Some provinces only allow a person to purchase a maximum supply of drugs at any one time, for example, 200-day supply. Ask your pharmacist at your local drug store or call your ministry of health to find out what is legally allowed in your province.

Passport

When travelling abroad, it is sometimes imperative that you have a passport. If you don't have one, then simply visit your local travel agency and ask for Form A. You will need two passport photos taken in a studio or photo booth, proof of citizenship and $60. Once processed, you should have your passport within five business days. Your passport is valid for five years.

Acceptable proof of citizenship is your birth certificate, or if you are from Quebec, your record of birth. For those born outside of Canada, you require a Canadian citizenship card.

Should you wish to obtain a passport while outside of Canada, simply contact a Canadian embassy or consulate and they will forward you the necessary documentation. Return the completed documentation and the embassy or consulate will courier it back to Canada for processing.

Citizenship Cards

Canadian citizens born outside the country may want to carry a wallet-sized citizenship identification card to assist with border crossings. If you wish to obtain a citizenship card, schedule an appointment with your local citizenship office and bring the following:

- certificate of Canadian citizenship

- two pieces of personal identification, like your driver's licence or social insurance card

- two wallet-sized photos taken at a studio or photo booth

- $75 processing fee

Citizenship cards are a valid form of identification and can currently be used when crossing the border to the United States in the absence of a passport. However, the time may come that you may require a passport to enter the United States.

Amendments to the U.S. Immigration Act, which became law as of September 1996, require stricter reporting requirements at U.S. border crossings. The United States wants to crack down on people who are staying longer in their country than legally permissible. One way to implement such a system is the mandatory scanning of passports. With the uncertainty regarding the implementation of the new U.S. immigration laws, it may be prudent to obtain a passport as soon as possible. The United States may impose this requirement with little notice, so take heed.

ABOUT THE AUTHORS

Tim Cestnick is a chartered accountant, and president of The WaterStreet Group Inc., based in Toronto. He writes a biweekly column for the *Globe and Mail,* spends a good portion of his time travelling our country speaking to investment advisors, employee groups, other chartered accountants, and the general public on the issue of taxation. He teaches for the Ontario Institute of Chartered Accountants, and is the author and a co-author of numerous books, including *A Declaration of Taxpayer Rights,* and *Your Family's Money* with Jerry White.

Carmen Da Silva is an Investment Tax Strategist with Dundee Wealth Management.

Barry Fish is with Fish and Associates, Barrister and Solicitors, 7951 Yonge Street, Thornhill, Ontario, L3T 2C4.

Brian Koscak, B.A. (Hon.), M.A., A.I.I.C., J.D., L.L.B., is a lawyer in Toronto. Brian has a joint law degree from both the University of Windsor and the University of Detroit Mercy School of Law where he earned his L.L.B. and J.D. in May 1997. Previously he received his M.A. in Judicial Administration and B.A. in Political Science, both from Brock University. Prior to attending law school, Brian worked for Medipac International Inc., one of Canada's largest providers of long-term travel insurance, as Director of Relationship Marketing. Brian was chiefly responsible for developing the CSA's membership benefits program and was actively involved in the CSA's Government and Lobby Committee. Brian has also been extensively involved in senior management positions within an insurance brokerage firm while working in the personal, commercial and employee benefits divisions of the company. Brian has obtained his designation as an Associate of the Insurance Institute of Canada (A.I.I.C.) and successfully completed his life, accident and sickness and insurance broker licenses in the province of Ontario.

Les Kotzer is with Fish and Associates, Barrister and Solicitors, 7951 Yonge Street, Thornhill, Ontario, L3T 2C4.

Harley Mintz, F.C.A., Managing Partner and Senior Tax Partner, Mintz and Partners, received his Bachelor of Commerce degree from the University of Toronto in 1972, his C.A. designation in 1975, his Fellowship of the Institute of Chartered Accountants in 1994, and his Chartered Financial Planner degree in 1997.

Harley specializes in financial and estate planning, syndications and offshore planning. He has written many articles on accounting and tax subjects for newspapers and has appeared frequently on the radio to discuss various tax issues. Harley has also lectured on taxation at the business school of York University, and on C.A. exam techniques for several international accounting firms and provincial Institutes of Chartered Accountants across Canada. He sits on the boards of several charitable foundations.

Kevyn Nightingale founded the International Tax Services Group in 1992. He is a graduate of the University of Toronto (BCom, 1985). He obtained his Chartered Accountant's designation in 1987. Mr. Nightingale completed the CICA In-Depth Tax Course in 1990 and obtained his CPA in 1994 (Illinois State Board of Accountancy).

Mr. Nightingale has lectured on Canadian and U.S. tax at York University, for the Institute of Chartered Accountants of Ontario, the Florida Bar and a number of other professional organizations. He served as co-chair of the PC Party of Ontario Finance and Taxation committee, and is co-chair of the policy committee of the Canadian Alliance. Kevyn has authored many articles on Canadian and U.S. tax, and is a regular contributor to *Tax Topics,* a weekly publication of CCH.

The International Tax Services Group is an association of tax practitioners. The practice is devoted to providing the best possible service to businesses and individuals who have an exposure to taxation in Canada and other countries. The group's principal activity is the provision of U.S. and cross-border taxation services to the legal and accounting professions, as well as the financial services industry. It plans for tax minimization, prepares returns, negotiates with tax authorities and provides litigation support. A large portion of the practice involves assisting individuals moving between the United States and Canada, and Canadian-based companies doing business in the United States. Currently, the group serves a clientele of over 200 accounting and law firms.

Gordon Polovin is an independent offshore investment expert and advisor.

Christopher Radomski, B.Sc., J.D., L.L.B., practices with the international firm of attorneys McLean McNally in the Turks and Caicos Islands, one of the largest offshore law firms, specializing in the areas of international tax and business planning for Canadian and American individuals and corporations.

Mr. Radomski possesses Canadian and American law degrees and is admitted to practice in the provinces of Ontario and British Columbia, as well as the Turks and Caicos Islands, where he currently holds the position of Secretary of the Bar Association.

Mr. Radomski has written many articles on the subject of offshore finance and has appeared as a guest speaker at conferences throughout North America. His areas of practice are tax and estate planning, asset protection, international business transactions, securities, and general corporate commercial law.

Mark Simone is currently the President of Medipac International Inc. and past Executive Director of the Canadian Snowbird Association. He is viewed as an authority on Canadian snowbirds, having been involved with the CSA from its inception. He has been interviewed and quoted numerous times in the media. Mark has been involved with seniors' issues for over a decade and is an avid promoter of active and healthy lifestyles after 50.

Prior to joining Medipac in 1992, Mark held senior executive positions in the travel and tourism industry. Mark's strengths are his negotiating and people skills. His recent accomplishments include creating and managing "Snowbird Extravaganza." This is a consumer trade show held annually in Tampa, Florida, in which over 320 exhibitors and more than 75,000 attendees participated in 1997.

Mark is married to his enchanting wife Linda and has two grown-up children, Damon and Jacqueline. They are also the proud grandparents of Jacqueline's daughter, Donna and are devoted to their dogs.

Jerry White is Canada's most widely recognized personal finance commentator. Born in Toronto, he received graduate level degrees from the University of Toronto, City University in London, England, and the International Management Centre in Buckingham, England. He has also taught in graduate business schools at the University of Toronto and New York University in New York City.

Jerry is the author/editor of over 40 business and finance books, including *Your Family's Money* and *What the Rich Do: What They Have and How They Keep It*. He is a frequent financial commentator on radio and television programs and conducts over 300 seminars in North America each year.